'Hands off—

Martyn's mouth [...]
just me that you [...]
you already have an ongoing attachment?'

His glance flicked over her, and she was suddenly aware of her femininity in a way that was utterly disturbing. Working with him was going to be fraught with danger; she could see it coming.

'I have no aversion to you, Dr Lancaster,' she said, striving to keep a steady tone. 'As to any attachment I might have, you can rest assured I won't let it interfere with the job.'

When **Joanna Neil** discovered Mills & Boon, her life-long addiction to reading crystallised into an exciting new career writing medical romances. Her characters are probably the outcome of her varied career, which includes working as a clerk, typist, nurse and infant teacher. She enjoys dressmaking and cooking at her Leicestershire home. Her family includes a husband, son and daughter, an exuberant yellow Labrador and two slightly crazed cockatiels.

LOVING REMEDY

BY
JOANNA NEIL

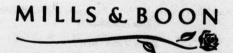

MILLS & BOON LIMITED
ETON HOUSE, 18–24 PARADISE ROAD
RICHMOND, SURREY, TW9 1SR

For Liam

MILLS & BOON, the Rose Device and LOVE ON CALL are trademarks of the publisher.

*First published in Great Britain 1995
by Mills & Boon Limited*

© Joanna Neil 1995

*Australian copyright 1995   Philippine copyright 1995
This edition 1995*

ISBN 0 263 79035 5

*Set in 10½ on 12½ pt Linotron Times
03-9504-48146*

*Typeset in Great Britain by Centracet, Cambridge
Made and printed in Great Britain*

CHAPTER ONE

'Now there's a man you'd be glad to have on your team.'

'Who's that, Dad?' Preoccupied, Sarah Prentiss gave a quick smile of thanks as her mother helped her to hoist her small son up the steps of the park's pavilion. When they were standing safely on the slabbed veranda, she glanced over to the expanse of green where a football match was in noisy progress.

'Tall fellow, running with the ball. Black hair.' Richard Moore removed his spectacles and gave them a vigorous wipe with the corner of a clean handkerchief, something Sarah had seen him do twice already this afternoon. It was on the tip of her tongue to quiz him about it when he replaced them on his nose and peered once more at the green. 'Can't miss him, girl. Even I could pick him out of a crowd. Look at that footwork. Did you see that goal? It's the second one he's banged in. I'd put money on who'd win that match.'

Sarah exchanged ruefully amused glances with her mother. Never an ardent football fan, she found it impossible to understand the feverish excitement that afflicted some men whenever a ball was being kicked about a field. She grinned at her father. 'Better save your money for the collection box,' she

5

advised him cheerfully. 'Or the sale in the club-house. The Friends of the Hospital need all the cash they can get for the new radiotherapy equipment they're trying to buy.'

'I wonder if he ever played professionally?' her father mused, his attention still caught up with the blue-shirted footballer.

Sarah followed the direction of his gaze, momentarily absorbing the swift action as the players raced between the posts. Whoever he was, he certainly made an impressive figure, even from a distance, though she couldn't help a faint stirring of relief that she didn't have to encounter all that hard muscle and athletic physique at closer quarters. It would be altogether too overpowering, she felt sure.

'I shouldn't think so,' she answered. 'It's a charity match—doctors versus Radiography is what I heard.'

It was good to see her father looking out with such animation over the heads of the crowd who had come to watch the game. It was a while now since he'd had the operation to put back in place the detached retina in his left eye, and, though everything had gone well and his sight seemed to be restored virtually to normal, Sarah couldn't quite manage to stem a slight feeling of anxiety.

There was nothing she could pin this feeling on to, and perhaps her professional training as a doctor should have made her more able to look at things from a cool, clinical viewpoint, but that ability seemed to have deserted her right now. He was her father and she loved him dearly, and her instinct for trouble, however unsoundly based, seemed to be working overtime where he was concerned.

At any rate, she was glad she'd made the decision to move back to her home town to be close to her family. Living fifty miles away had meant that she had only been able to come over once a fortnight, sandwiching her visits into her work schedule. That was behind her now, thankfully. She had her work as a locum to keep her going for the time being, and if things turned out well at her interview at the health centre next week she would have a more certain future to look forward to.

Whatever happened, she was staying. It would be good for Daniel, too. Hopefully, he'd be more settled, and he'd soon be wallowing in the affection of his grandparents.

'C'mon, Mummy.'

Feeling the impatient tug of her son's hand in hers, she realised that he was fast becoming restless while she was wool-gathering. She released him and watched as he ran through the opened glass doors into the pavilion. He was a sturdy three-year-old, and she felt a strong maternal pride swelling in her breast as she followed his quick, eager movements. Cool October sunlight slanted in through the windows, and danced off the bright, fair silk of his hair.

He seemed happy enough, Sarah told herself. Perhaps the loss of his father had not affected him as deeply as she had feared. A swift pang of anguish swept in on the tail of that thought. How many times had she asked herself that question in the last two years?

Daniel stopped and looked around with curiosity, and in no time at all had spied the counter with its carefully stacked displays of canned drinks and snacks.

'Juice,' he pronounced with characteristic strength of purpose. He looked at her. 'Juice, Mummy.'

Sarah turned to her parents. 'Shall we go in and get something to drink? I promised Jenny I'd help out with serving teas as soon as the rush from the sale started, and it looks as though that could be any time in the next half-hour.'

'Of course, darling.' Martha followed her grandson into the glass-walled pavilion and deposited her bags on a chair by the window. 'I'm parched. Will this table do, Richard? You can watch the match from here while Sarah and I see to the drinks.'

'That was a foul, an outright foul.' Intent on the game, Richard sat down and squinted crossly at the goings-on outside. Daniel scrambled up on to his knee.

'What's fow-ul, Grandad?'

Sarah and her mother left them to it and walked over to the counter.

'I'm so glad you could make it, Sarah,' Jenny said as they organised the refreshments. She was a vivacious girl, with a mass of black curly hair that refused to stay confined behind her cap whenever she was on duty in Casualty. The women had met when Sarah had put in a stint in the department just a couple of weeks ago. 'We shall need all the hands we can get once the initial sale fever dies down.'

'There's a good turn-out,' Sarah said reflectively, gazing out to scan the throng milling around the clubhouse a few hundred yards away.

Jenny nodded. 'There usually is for fund-raising events like this one, and people are very generous. Over the last few years we've managed to raise enough money for a scanner. And everyone we've asked for help has been happy to give us what time they can spare. We didn't have any trouble signing up the doctors for the football match, even though they'll have to dig deep in their pockets too. The winning team are pledged to donate a tenner each, and the losers are to give fifteen.'

'My father's picked out the best player. Apparently he's scored twice already.'

Jenny nodded. 'Yes, I've been watching. That's Martyn. He could score again if he'd only take me seriously.' She rolled her eyes dramatically and Sarah smiled.

'Like that, is it?'

'Oh, our Dr Lancaster is a real heart-throb. I'd take him on any day. Mind you, the competition's stiff. The nursing staff have just secretly nominated him this year's most eligible bachelor.' She sent a glance over the counter and the pastries stacked there. 'I guess I'll just have to beat them back with the left-over buns.'

Sarah laughed.

In a way, she envied Jenny. She couldn't remem-

ber ever being that bowled over by a man, except
perhaps in the very beginning with Colin. But that
seemed like a long time ago and she didn't suppose
there was a man born who could set her pulses
racing now. Perhaps she'd always been too serious,
too intent on her studies and her career. She was
guarded about her feelings these days. She had put
her emotions on the back burner for such a long
time, and she'd grown too wary of being hurt.

Martha slid a tea-cake on to a plate. 'If there's
going to be a bun-fight,' she said with a smile, 'I'll
take this to your dad now. I wouldn't like him to
miss out.'

'Is he OK, Mum?' Sarah sent a troubled look in
her mother's direction as they loaded up a tray and
moved away from the counter. 'I know he says he is,
but I can't help feeling that something's not quite
right.'

'You've noticed too, have you?' Martha's
expression was sombre. 'I don't know what to do,
Sarah. He won't tell me anything, just keeps fobbing
me off, saying I shouldn't fuss so, but I'm sure
something's wrong. He's such a stubborn man. I'm
sure if I hadn't badgered him to go and see a
specialist when he kept bumping into things he'd
have left it until it was too late. I'm so afraid the
same thing might be happening again.'

'It isn't likely, Mum.' Sarah tried to be reassuring.
'The operation was very successful. But I will try to
pick a good time to have a quiet word with him and

see if I can find out exactly what's happening. I know it's hard, but try not to worry.'

They went back to the table and Sarah passed a packet of biscuits across to Daniel before placing cups on the smooth laminated surface.

'Here you are, Dad,' she said. 'A nice hot cup of tea to keep the cold at bay.'

He took a sip and promptly screwed up his face. 'Not one drop of medicinal brandy in it, and you a doctor, too.'

Sarah chuckled as she sat down, and then disconcertingly found herself to be the object of a quietly piercing scrutiny.

'You should do that more often, my girl,' Richard said. She looked at him in puzzlement and he went on, 'A smile lights up your whole face.' He gazed at her intently. 'You can be a real stunner at times, you know, with that perfect bone-structure and those lovely green eyes. You get them from your mother. Not the hair, though. That fair hair comes from my side of the family. Makes you look ethereal, somehow. Fragile.'

'Goodness, Dad.' Sarah's tea nearly went down the wrong way. 'What brought this on?'

'It's true,' he said gruffly. He seemed to be studying every detail of her face, almost as though he wanted to memorise each and every one. 'Sometimes, when I look at you, I can hardly believe you're a fully qualified doctor, let alone a mother. You look so young.'

'Heavens, I'm twenty-nine, you know. Practically an old-timer.'

'You'll be that when you reach my age.' He finished off his tea and looked across at Martha. 'I'd like to go and see the finish of the match. Do you want to come along with me, or are you staying here with Daniel?'

'Swings,' Daniel said firmly, wriggling to the floor.

'Hmm.' Martha glanced at the boy. 'That's not a bad idea. I'll take Fidget-bottom over to the swings and give Sarah a chance to get on with serving her teas. We can meet back here later.'

Richard nodded. 'Suits me. I'll take a look in the sale-room when the game's over, see if there's any fishing tackle on offer.'

Daniel was already pulling at Martha's skirt, and when they headed for the doors a few minutes later Sarah took herself over to the counter to help out with the customers who were beginning to come through the doors in a steady stream. They were hungry and thirsty and she was kept busy for the next half-hour with scarcely a moment to catch her breath.

'I'll clear the debris from some of the tables,' Jenny said. 'We're running out of crockery.'

There was no doubting when the football match came to an end, because there was a sudden rush of people into the pavilion, and many of them had to take their drinks outside to avoid the crush.

Refilling the large teapot with hot water from the urn, Sarah paused to push back a wayward strand of hair from her temple. Glancing out of the window, she was just in time to see Daniel racing after another boy, and witness the heated altercation that followed as soon as he caught up with him. It looked as though they were fighting over the ownership of a balloon, and Martha was doing her best to sort it out. Sarah suppressed a grimace. Why was he always getting into scrapes of one sort or another? Hadn't she always tried to do her best to bring him up properly?

'Don't you think you should keep your mind on what you're doing?'

The deep masculine tones dragged her attention rapidly back to the pavilion and the owner of the voice. Her stare was met by a pair of cool blue eyes, and her hand faltered on the tap of the urn. It was the startling colour of those eyes that threw her mind off key for a moment, with their unusual jewelled brilliance, but when you added to that a smooth, wide brow and a clean-cut angular jawline it was hardly any wonder that she had trouble keeping her mouth from dropping open. She could quite well see why the nurses had nominated him the most eligible bachelor of the year. If you were judging by looks alone, that was. The crisp black hair that framed his head was expertly cut so that even after a strenuous game of football there wasn't a hair out of place.

He reached over the counter to turn off the tap and she looked down in dismay at the almost brimming teapot.

'That's how accidents happen,' he said curtly. 'Through not keeping your mind on the job.'

'I was about to turn it off,' she returned coolly, annoyed with herself for that momentary lapse of concentration. Now he'd probably get to thinking that he was the cause of it. From what Jenny had said, he had more than enough female admiration heaped his way to plant in his mind the idea that he was God's gift to womankind.

'Then it's a pity your reactions weren't a bit faster. You might have been scalded.'

'Thank you,' she said, 'for your timely intervention, though I can assure you it was quite unnecessary. I was keeping track of what's going on outside, but I was perfectly well aware of the tap running.' She gave the pot a purposeful stir and went on with what she thought was commendable politeness in the circumstances. 'Did you want a drink? Tea? Coffee? I do have a queue waiting.'

He scanned the counter and the neatly packaged snacks. Hearing shouts from outside, Sarah surreptitiously glanced out of the window again, and was horrified to see that Daniel was now engaged in a full-blown scrap, fists flying. For the second time this afternoon she wondered if she had gone wrong somewhere. She'd tried to keep his life well-ordered and secure, but with no father on the scene it hadn't been easy.

A sigh hovered faintly on her lips. It had been this time of year when Colin had died, but Daniel wouldn't remember that, would he? It was just she who had to face the memories, and they were always stronger when the autumn leaves started to fall.

'Tea will be fine. If it's no trouble, of course. I'd hate to put you out in any way.'

The edge of sarcasm wasn't lost on her, but she was saved from replying by Jenny's appearance on the scene, a precariously heaped tray in her hands.

'Let me help you with that,' Martyn Lancaster said, removing the burden from her and placing it on an empty stretch of counter. 'How's my favourite girl? It must be all of two weeks since I saw you last.'

Sarah poured the tea and pushed the cup towards him.

'Two weeks, four days and——' Jenny did a swift calculation on her fingers '—eighteen hours.' She clapped a hand over her mouth. 'Oh, dear, am I making myself too obvious?' She was grinning behind her palm, and his mouth crooked in amusement as he slid a hand around her waist.

'Delightfully,' he said, and she removed her hand in time to receive the firm kiss he planted on her mouth.

Sarah just managed to stop herself from pulling a face and turned to the next customer. How these gullible women could fall for a man as arrogant as he obviously was she had no idea. As far as she was concerned, the lady-killing Dr Lancaster was just the sort of man she'd move heaven and earth to avoid.

'Can I help you?' she asked, dealing with the

people waiting patiently in line, and after a few more minutes found that the rush had at last died down and she could gather her thoughts once more.

'How much do I owe you?'

She turned her head and gazed blankly for a moment at Dr Lancaster, amazed to find that he was still there. Jenny had gone off again, to clear more tables. 'I beg your pardon?'

'For the tea. You surely didn't imagine I was referring to your abundant charm?'

'I thought you had more than enough of that for both of us.'

'And you have a very sharp tongue.'

'I'm not used to being spoken to as though I'm a lackey who doesn't come up to scratch,' Sarah told him sharply, 'and I don't take kindly to being criticised by someone I've never even met before. I'm here as a volunteer, not as a whipping-boy for your ill temper.'

His eyes narrowed. 'I'm a doctor. It bothers me when I see potentially dangerous situations that could be avoided, but. . .maybe I over-reacted. And I can see how busy you've been.' He fished in his pocket and threw some coins on to the counter. 'That should cover it, I think.' He studied her thoughtfully. 'Perhaps we got off to a wrong start. You're new around here, aren't you? I don't remember seeing you about the hospital. Not that I'm there all the time—far from it—but I do manage to get to know most of the staff after a while.'

'I've only been here a few weeks. In the city, I

mean. I'm working as a locum while I get myself settled.'

'That accounts for why we haven't met before this.' He glanced at her obliquely, his gaze slanting over her slender figure in the neat emerald skirt and soft cotton blouse. 'I hadn't realised that you're a doctor too. Somehow I'd imagined that you might be a nurse, or. . . Well, it doesn't matter. My apologies. If you need anyone to show you around the place, I'd be only too happy to oblige.'

Sarah stiffened, schooling her features into a cool, dismissive smile. 'I can manage, thank you.' She'd seen that stirring of interest in a man's eyes before, and he needn't think she'd fall into line along with the others. Good heavens, not ten minutes ago he'd been all over Jenny. 'I've lived away for a while,' she said. 'But this is my home town and I'm well-acquainted with what's on offer.' Her tone was cool and she gave him a look which she hoped would convey a deeper meaning. If he too was on offer, she wasn't interested.

He frowned, and whatever he might have said was lost as Daniel came running in. Stopping short at Martyn's feet, he tipped his head back and looked up at them both. Always quick to sense an atmosphere, he stared hardest at Martyn Lancaster, his chin jutting belligerently.

'Who are you?' he demanded to know. 'Go away. My mummy doesn't want to know you.'

'Daniel!' Sarah's gasp floated on the air between

them. 'That was very rude. Say you're sorry, at once.'

'Shan't.' Daniel's mouth set in an obstinate line and he turned around and stamped out of the pavilion, bumping into a harassed Martha as he went. She took his hand and led him firmly away, admonishing him as they retreated down the steps.

Sarah swallowed hard. 'I'm very sorry about that,' she said to Martyn. 'I must apologise for my son. He doesn't usually behave as badly as that. I can't think what's got into him.'

Martyn's eyes narrowed on the third finger of her left hand, noting the gold ring. 'I hadn't realised you were married,' he said. 'My mistake. As to your son, perhaps he's the reason you're so distracted. I see now why you were gazing out of the window. Perhaps you should take him in hand before his behaviour affects your work and has more serious consequences than it might have had earlier this afternoon.'

Her sharp intake of breath went unnoticed as a sudden scream and the horrible sound of wailing started up outside the building. Sarah froze while Jenny went to investigate. A few moments later she returned, saying breathlessly, 'Martyn, can you come? We need a doctor. A child's hurt—something to do with a swing, I think.'

He was already moving to the door, the pair of them disappearing from view down the concrete steps and heading for the play area.

Sarah went suddenly pale and began to feel sick.

Not Daniel. Please let it not be Daniel. Then her automatic reflexes took over and her professional training came into play. She reached for the first-aid box from under the counter and hurried outside.

A little boy lay crumpled on the hard ground in front of a swing, and as she took in the clothes he was wearing—blue jeans and a red sweater—she felt a surge of relief that it was not her son. The child was conscious and crying pitifully and it was clear that he was in quite a lot of pain.

'What's happened here, young man?' Martyn asked softly, kneeling down beside him.

'F-fell off. Some—someone pushed me.'

'Oh, dear.' He made a swift initial examination as the boy lay still, his large hands moving delicately over the child's spine. 'And what's your name?'

'Ch-Christian.'

The child's mother was clearly upset. A tawny-haired woman, she crouched down on the ground beside her son and tried not to let him see how anxious she was. 'Someone ran by the swing,' she said. 'Knocked him flying.'

Sarah looked around and saw that Daniel was standing quietly at the front of the little crowd that was gathering. He looked pale and subdued, his cheek huddled into Martha's skirt.

'Wasn't me,' he said, and his face crumpled as though he was about to cry too. He knuckled his eyes and Martha's arm went around him.

'Of course it wasn't you, sweetheart. You weren't anywhere near him.'

'Can you sit up?' Martyn was saying. 'I'd like to take a look at you. I'll be as quick as I can.'

Sarah fixed her attention on them once more, noting how gentle he was as he carefully examined the boy. The child had fallen awkwardly and was obviously in shock.

'How old are you, Christian?' Martyn asked. 'Five?'

The boy struggled to stop his tears. 'I'm four,' he said. 'It hurts. It hurts a lot.'

'I bet it does. You're a very brave lad.' To the mother he added, 'I think he fell directly on to his shoulder and he's fractured his collarbone. It's quite a common injury in youngsters, nothing to be unduly worried about. At this age, children's bones mend quite easily. What we have to do now is to put his arm in a sling to make him more comfortable, then we'll take him over to Casualty so that they can take a look at him.'

Sarah came forward with the first-aid box and proffered a roll of bandage. He took it, glancing at her briefly. 'Thanks.' Turning back to the boy, he made a neat triangular sling, his movements quick and efficient, then he asked, 'Does that feel a bit better?'

The boy nodded slowly, and Martyn said, 'You might find putting your head a little to the side helps make it feel easier. Like this.'

Carefully, he demonstrated, and the boy relaxed a little. 'Yes,' he said. 'But it still hurts.'

'I know. The doctor in Casualty will probably give

you something to take the pain away.' Getting to his feet, he told the mother, 'We'll go over there now. They'll probably advise that he keep the sling on for three or four weeks.' Helping the boy to stand, he added with mock-sternness, 'That means there'll be no tree-climbing for you for a while.'

Christian managed a weak smile and Jenny said, 'Shall I take him? It's no trouble.'

Martyn shook his head. 'I'm going that way. I said I'd call in at the hospital later this afternoon. Some notes I need to collect.'

They watched as the trio went off towards the car park, and when the small crowd had thinned out Jenny said, 'He's always been good with children. When he sees them in the clinic he always manages to get a smile out of them.'

'What does he do at the hospital?' Sarah wanted to know. She was hoping she hadn't been at logger-heads with one of their top consultants, since she might have to deal with him again at some time in the future during the course of her work, but it wasn't very likely. Most consultants she had come across were in their late forties, and she wouldn't have put Dr Lancaster much above thirty-five.

'He sees patients at the orthopaedic clinic, one morning and one afternoon a week,' Jenny answered. 'He specialised for a while, but then he decided he would prefer to work as a GP. I think he's been doing that now for around six years—he's a partner in a practice—but he still likes to keep in touch with hospital life, hence the clinic.'

'He's a GP?' Sarah echoed. Her mind was suddenly locked into overdrive. Of course, his being in general practice wouldn't affect her in any way, would it? There wasn't much chance that they would ever come into contact with each other again, was there? Especially if she managed to land this job at the health centre. Why, then, was she suddenly assailed by doubt?

'Yes,' Jenny said cheerfully. 'In the north-east of the county. In fact, I think the practice is near to where you're living right now. A lovely spot, close to the river. The Soar Bridge Health Centre. Do you know it?'

Sarah's spirits plummeted to an all-time low. Inwardly she groaned. Oh, she knew it well enough. Why, oh, why did it have to be the very place where she had applied for a job?

CHAPTER TWO

IT WAS raining on the day that she was to go for her interview. A wind was blowing and the trees that lined the avenue where she lived in her tidy, white-fronted cottage were shedding their leaves with gusto. Sarah wondered at first if that wasn't some kind of depressing omen, and then gave herself a severe telling-off. She wanted this job, and she was going to do her darnedest to get it, despite Martyn Lancaster. Bother him for filling her with self-doubt.

He wasn't the man who had written to her, inviting her to come along, after all. It had been the senior partner, Dr John Stokes, who had done that, and with any luck she would manage to impress him and convince him that she was the one for the job despite any objections Dr Lancaster might come up with.

Martha had offered to look after Daniel for her while she went to the centre, and she took him into the warmth of her mother's homely kitchen, taking off her damp scarf and giving it a shake.

'Will this rain never end?' she said to Martha. 'Three days it's been like this. I'd forgotten what it's like in this neck of the woods.'

'Best stay put by the fire in this weather,' Richard commented, looking up from the paper he'd been reading.

Martha's green eyes sparkled with sympathetic amusement. 'Well, you can dry off a bit here before you have to go out again. There's tea in the pot. Help yourself.'

'It's good of you to have Daniel like this,' Sarah said, sitting down. 'I don't mean to keep asking you, because I know you're busy enough with your own job. I've enrolled him at the local nursery school and I've taken on a new nanny to take care of him when I have to be on duty.' She helped Daniel out of his coat, a difficult operation since he insisted on holding on tightly to his battered teddy bear. 'See if you can find the jigsaw puzzle you were doing last week,' she suggested to him, and he went off happily to search in the cupboard under the stairs. 'I hope it works out all right,' she told Martha. 'He didn't seem too thrilled at the prospect, but she's a nice girl and her references were very good.'

'I'm sure he'll settle, given time. He's had a few changes in his short life, and it's bound to take a while for him to adjust. As for my job, it's only a few hours a week, after all, and it isn't exactly strenuous, doing something I love. I'm just happy they actually pay me to teach cookery.'

Sarah managed a smile, then said, 'Even so, after the way he behaved last week, I was worried that he might be too much of a handful. I can't think what got into him.'

'Who can tell? He's a bright lad, though, and he was taking an awful lot of interest in the menfolk around, and asking some pretty direct questions.'

Sarah looked at her mother intently. 'About what? Colin?' Martha nodded, and Sarah went on thoughtfully, 'You wouldn't think he'd remember his daddy all that clearly, would you? He was only eighteen months old at the time.'

'I'm not sure that he does,' Martha said. 'I think it's more likely the fact that other children have one and he doesn't, and he wonders why.'

'Things hardly ever seem to work out quite the way we want them to, do they?'

She'd been dazzled by Colin when she had first met him. Fair-haired and grey-eyed, he'd been tall and lean and had a quirky sense of humour that she had found intriguing at the time. He'd been a pharmacist at the hospital where she was finishing off her clinical sciences course, and she'd thought him steady and dependable, the sort of man she'd like to spend the rest of her life with. They'd married as soon as she qualified, and for a while they'd been happy, engrossed in each other. It was only later that the cracks had started to appear.

'I must go,' she said, getting to her feet. 'Is there anything I can fetch for you from the shops while I'm out?'

'Some fresh yeast from the bakery, if you would. I need it for my bread class tomorrow.'

'Will do. I'll be off, then.'

'See you later, love.' Her father's voice was faintly abstracted and she looked across the room at him. He was shifting his paper about and squinting irritably.

'Is anything wrong, Dad? Are you not seeing as well as you should?'

'It's these wretched glasses,' he muttered. 'Forever need cleaning.'

'Don't you think you should see the specialist again?' Sarah urged. 'If you're having any problems at all, you should let him know.'

'I'm not having any problems, girl. I told you that last week. I'm perfectly all right. It's just my glasses pick up every speck of dust around. There's no need for everyone to keep fussing this way, getting into a tizzy over nothing. I'm fine.'

'You've not had any more sparks or flashes or any black curtain to stop you from seeing properly?'

'Nothing like that at all. It's my age, if anything. You don't expect to see as clearly as you used to at my time of life.'

Sarah wasn't having any of that. 'You're retired, Dad, not in your dotage yet. I think you should give the specialist a ring and make an appointment to see him.'

'I already have an appointment, in January.'

'But you don't have to wait that long,' she persisted. 'Let me arrange it for you.'

'We'll see.'

Sarah opened her mouth to say something and he put in firmly, 'I'm not saying yes, I'm not saying no. I'll think about it. That's my last word on the subject. Now you go off to that interview and show 'em you're the best.'

There was no point in pushing the subject further

right now, she could see that. Buttoning up her beige-coloured raincoat, she made for the door.

'Good luck,' Martha said.

'Thanks. I'll probably need it.'

'Nonsense. You're a brilliant doctor, and I'm sure that Dr Lancaster will be bound to recognise it. He seemed very warm and friendly, and very competent, I thought.'

'There wasn't a lot of warmth coming my way, Mum. He and I didn't really hit it off, you know. Still, there may be other partners whose opinions count for more than his.'

She kept her fingers crossed on the steering-wheel all the way to the main street of the village which housed the health centre. More than anything she wanted this job.

She'd seen the place some years back, before Dr Lancaster had made his appearance, and it was a fairly new building, attractively designed to be pleasing on the eye, with plenty of windows and warm-looking red tiles on the roof. A new wing had been built on in recent years, she'd heard, and there was a feeling of spaciousness throughout. A shrubbery had been planted, along with a herbaceous border, and there were mature trees in the background. On the south side, the land dipped to a slow-moving river, and the huge weeping willow that trailed its branches in the water could be seen from the waiting-room window. Her own home wasn't more than four miles away, and the hours that had been mentioned would suit her and Daniel perfectly.

Glancing at her watch, she saw that she had a few minutes to spare. Time enough to pop in to the bakery and pick up the yeast for her mother. The shops were right next to the health centre, with a pharmacy on the corner and the bakery next door. She parked her Metro neatly and went to make her purchase.

It was still raining and the pavement was slippery with damp leaves. As she came out of the shop she noticed an elderly woman making her way along the street, her shoes a little loose at the heel. The woman turned as something caught her eye in a shop window, and even as Sarah started to call a warning her heel tipped sideways, sliding across the wet ground, and the woman began to fall. It all happened so fast that no one was able to do anything to stop the sequence of events, and the frail-looking woman was sprawled on the pavement within seconds.

It took Sarah a moment to get to her. 'Are you hurt?' she asked.

The woman's face was twisted with pain, and for a minute or two she didn't speak, but just held her breath and clutched at her ankle.

'It feels as though it's broken,' she managed at last. 'My ankle. I twisted it as I fell.'

'I'm a doctor,' Sarah said. 'May I take a look? Do you hurt anywhere else?'

'Please, if you wouldn't mind. Thank you very much. It's so kind of you. It was so silly, such a silly thing to happen. And so quickly, too.' The white-faced pensioner took a deep breath. 'It's just my ankle.'

Kneeling down beside her, Sarah slid the shoe from the injured foot and felt carefully around the painful area, trying not to cause any more discomfort.

'There's some swelling,' she said at last, 'but I don't think anything's broken. An ice-pack will take some of the swelling down and make it feel easier and then it can be bandaged to help you feel more comfortable. You'll need to rest the foot as much as possible, and perhaps raise it up with a cushion for support. Is there anyone at home who can look after you, Mrs. . .?'

'Benson.' The old lady shook her head. 'My Harry passed away over ten years ago. But my neighbour's very good to me. I could ask her if she'd mind getting me a few bits in till I'm myself again.'

'We'll see if we can get things sorted out for you. You can take aspirin or paracetamol for the pain, whichever suits you best. At least you did this in the right place,' Sarah commented with a smile. 'The health centre's only round the corner. The people in there will look after you.' Helping her to her feet, she put a supporting arm to her back and said, 'Lean on me. I'll see that you get there safely.'

'You're very kind,' the woman said again. 'I am feeling a bit shaky. I'm just a trouble to everyone, and. . . Oh, dear, look at your coat; I've made you get it all dirty.'

Sarah glanced down at her raincoat, unhappily

noting the damp grey streaks where it had trailed on the ground as she'd knelt down.

'You mustn't worry about that, ' she murmured, inwardly wincing at the fates which had made her look thoroughly dishevelled on a day when she had desperately wanted to be seen at her best. Not only that, but a glance at her watch told her she was late, too. 'It couldn't be helped,' she said matter-of-factly. 'I dare say it will clean up well enough, and you're not a trouble to anyone.'

They approached the building and Sarah added, 'I think your shoes might have been part of the reason for your fall, you know. Are they a little loose?'

'They are a bit, now you come to mention it. One of them keeps slipping up and down at the back.'

'You could try a heel-grip. That might make it a better fit and safer for you to wear.'

'I hadn't thought of that. Of course, you're probably right.'

They had reached the main doors now, and Sarah took the woman inside and explained to the receptionist what had happened.

'Would you get someone to look at her? She's a bit shocked after her fall, and she'll need an ice-pack and then a support bandage. I'm Sarah Prentiss, by the way. You were expecting me?'

'Ah, yes.' The receptionist looked at her with curiosity. 'We were wondering what had happened to you. I'll let Dr Stokes know that you've arrived just as soon as I've taken Mrs Benson to the nurse.'

To the pale-faced Mrs Benson, she said, 'Don't you worry, dear. We'll take good care of you.'

Just then the door to the waiting-room opened and Martyn Lancaster walked in. He looked completely different from the way she remembered him, and it was almost a shock to her senses to see him dressed in formal clothes, a beautifully cut grey suit and immaculate thinly striped shirt. He wore a tie, in a matching grey with tiny flecks of colour. The impact was a powerful one and her mouth went a little dry as she stared at him. She wasn't quite sure why he should provoke such a strong awareness in her, but it was certainly there, and she could only put it down to another facet of her general tension this afternoon.

He was startled to see her, that was plain to see, but when the receptionist hastened to tell him, 'This is Dr Prentiss,' he merely nodded.

'We've already met.'

The girl looked a little taken aback by the curtness of his tone, but she recovered quickly enough and led Mrs Benson away, leaving the two of them alone in the waiting-room.

Dr Lancaster's hard blue glance skated over her from top to toe, taking in the dirt-spattered raincoat, and Sarah felt the heat rising in her cheeks.

'So you made it here at last,' he said. 'We'd just about given up on you.' It was plain that he wasn't at all pleased at having been kept waiting.

'I'm sorry I'm late,' she began.

'Did you have trouble finding the place?'

'No. I used to live hereabouts, so I more or less know my way around. The new by-pass confused me when I first came back to the area, but I think I've just about sorted out the changes.'

'You haven't been in an accident?' He glanced once more at her grubby coat, his dark brows meeting in a frown. 'Driving conditions can be hazardous in this weather, especially if there's mud from the construction works spilling on to the main road.'

'No, nothing like that. The roads really weren't too bad. I——'

His head was inclined in grim acknowledgement. 'Then perhaps I should tell you, Mrs Prentiss,' he cut in, 'that we place a high value on punctuality in this practice. Our patients are entitled to expect an efficient service from us, and that includes doing our best to ensure that they are not kept waiting any longer than is absolutely necessary.'

Sarah's shoulders went back at his implied criticism. 'I should have thought that goes without saying, Dr Lancaster. I pride myself on my time-keeping, but occasionally there are circumstances which can cause unavoidable delays. But perhaps you feel that I should have kept my appointment with you and Dr Stokes regardless of the fact that Mrs Benson had fallen and was in some distress? Or would you have preferred it if I'd simply left her lying on the pavement for someone else to deal with?'

Her hands tightened into fists against the fabric of

her coat, while her eyes glittered with angry resentment. The man was so determined to find fault with her that he hadn't given her a chance to explain. She had been right in her very first assessment of him. He was arrogant beyond belief.

'I don't follow your line of reasoning,' he said abruptly. 'What's this about Mrs Benson?'

'If you hadn't been so intent on jumping to conclusions, you wouldn't have had any trouble at all in following me.' She gritted her teeth and went on tautly, 'I was late because I saw Mrs Benson fall in the street and stopped to help. That also accounts for why I'm looking less than presentable at this moment. My apologies for that, Dr Lancaster.'

As soon as her outburst was over, she realised with sinking spirits that she could probably say goodbye to any hope of getting this job. There was something about this man that drew out the worst in her, and it was her own fault now if she paid the price for her momentary lack of control. She had let her tongue get the better of her and that was a stupid thing to do when so much was at stake.

'You have a temper, Mrs Prentiss.' He sent her a coolly speculative look. 'Unexpected, given your fair, fragilely feminine appearance. But then, looks can be deceptive. Do you usually have a problem containing it? Because, if so, that might lead you into trouble. Some of our patients can be difficult at times—not intentionally, of course, but illness affects people in all kinds of ways, and it could be disastrous if you aren't able at least to appear in command of yourself.'

Sarah's chin went up. 'I may look "fragile," as you put it, but I'm hardly wet behind the ears as well. I have been in general practice before this, and I've had plenty of opportunity to deal with fractious and demanding patients without in any way losing my cool.'

'You don't look old enough to have had that much experience.'

His blunt comment rankled, as it was probably meant to do, and she bit back a swift retort as the door to the waiting-room opened and John Stokes walked in. She had probably cooked her goose already, but it would be sheer folly to reduce it to cinders.

'Dr Prentiss—Sarah, isn't it? May I call you that? Our receptionist told me that you'd arrived.'

Dr Stokes took her hand in his and gave it a welcoming shake. He was a lean man of medium height, with brown hair greying at the temples, though it was still surprisingly dark, and his hazel eyes held a friendly sparkle. He looked to be somewhere in his early sixties, but his facial bone-structure was strong, and Sarah judged that in his youth he must have been a handsome man. She took to him instantly, recognising the inherent warmth and compassion that emanated from him. He was a man people would trust and confide in.

'I see Martyn has already been getting to know you. Good, good.' He nodded approval. 'Our other colleague, James, is out on his rounds at the moment, but I expect you'll meet him later. We have to thank you, I hear, for looking after one of our patients. She's a frail soul. Lives alone in one of the bungalows on the outskirts of the village. At least she won't have to be climbing any stairs.'

'Is she all right?' Sarah asked.

'She'll be fine. She's a bit shocked, but the girls are giving her a cup of tea. Would you care for one, my dear? There's a tray ready in my office if you'd like to come through.'

'I expect Dr Prentiss would like time to tidy up and compose herself after her mission of mercy,' Martyn suggested, and Sarah was so astonished by this unexpected gesture of consideration that she sent him a quick look from under her gold lashes.

He lifted a brow in recognition of her unvoiced doubts, but it seemed his thoughtfulness was genuine, and she said evenly, 'Thank you. I'd be glad of a few minutes.'

John Stokes smiled in agreement. 'Of course, you go along. My office is just through that green door. Join us when you're ready.'

'I'll show you where you can freshen up.' Martyn's fingers closed around her arm as he drew her towards the wash-room, and for a few seconds she was aware of an oddly disturbing tremor which ran through her limbs and ended with a peculiar fluttering of nerves in her stomach. It was tension, she reasoned. Quite a natural reaction in the circumstances, now that her mind was back on course for the coming interview and the adrenalin had begun flowing.

He left her alone in the room, where she quickly removed her coat and applied a damp tissue to clean off the worst of the splashes. She was wearing a smart suit in a beautiful shade of sea-green linen that seemed to reflect and emphasise the colour of her eyes in a pleasing way. Beneath the jacket she had on a cream silk blouse with a collar delicately embroidered in matching tones. Running a comb through her shining, almost shoulder-length hair, she teased it into place, then lightly touched up her make-up. Looking at herself in the mirror, she hoped fervently that Dr Lancaster would find nothing amiss with her appearance this time.

At last, satisfied that she had done all she could to make herself look tidy, she headed for Dr Stokes's office.

'There you are, my dear,' he greeted her. 'Come in, and take a seat.' He waved a hand towards a buttoned leather chair opposite.

She sat, aware that Dr Lancaster remained standing over by the window. The blue eyes had taken stock of her as soon as she had entered the room, and for no accountable reason she felt uncomfortably warm under that steady appraisal.

'Will you have tea?' Dr Stokes asked, but she refused politely. With Dr Lancaster watching her like a hawk, she couldn't be sure that her hand wouldn't develop a fit of the shakes, and she wasn't about to take any more risks. His effect on her was beginning to be alarming.

Dr Stokes removed a digestive biscuit from a plate on his desk, and for a moment she thought he was about to dunk it. He must have had second thoughts, though, for with a glimmer of amusement in his eyes he said, 'Perhaps I'd better not,' and slid it on to his saucer. 'We'll make a start, shall we?'

Sarah's lips curved in an answering smile. She liked John Stokes. In some as yet indefinable way he reminded her of her father.

'My wife has been part of the practice for many years now,' Dr Stokes explained, 'but she's retiring to take a well-earned rest, potter about the garden and do all the things she's always wanted to do. I shall be joining her myself in the new year. Martyn will take over then as senior partner, and he'll sort out a replacement for myself.' Sarah's insides took a downward turn at this casually thrown in piece of information, but she tried not to let any of her emotions show as Dr Stokes continued, 'In the meantime, we do need a woman to join us. Perhaps you could tell us a little about yourself?' He had her application form in front of him. 'I can see that you're exceptionally well-qualified. You're working as a locum at present, I understand?'

'I am.' She told him a little about the variety of work she'd encountered, in the hospital and in the numerous practices in the town. 'I've recently moved to the area to be nearer to my parents, and I took on the locum work to tide me over while I settle in.

Before that I worked part-time in a large suburban practice.'

Dr Stokes was sifting through some papers on his desk. 'Yes, I have your references here. They're excellent.' He passed them to Martyn. 'It seems your colleagues really didn't want to lose you.'

'It was a difficult choice to make, but my father hasn't been well, and I wanted to be on hand. Neither of my parents is getting any younger.'

'I can see how you would be torn.'

John Stokes was sympathising when Martyn cut in abrasively with, 'So what can you offer us, Mrs Prentiss—Sarah?'

Clearly, he didn't want to waste time observing any niceties, and Sarah replied succinctly, 'Obstetrics and gynaecology are my special interests, with menopausal problems and HRT among them. I've also had quite a lot of experience in paediatrics.'

'And have you kept yourself up to date with current ideas?'

'Of course.'

'How?'

He'd hardly given her time to take a breath before he posed the curt question, but she was determined not to let his harsh manner undermine her confidence. She said calmly, 'I've been on several courses over the past few years, Dr Lancaster, and I make a point of reading the literature that comes with the post.'

'You said you worked part-time. Presumably that was to fit in with the demands of your child?'

'That's right.'

'The hours you'll be required to work here will be somewhat longer than you're used to. This practice is hard work, and certainly isn't for the faint-hearted. We've a growing community to tend, and we need commitment. Are you up to it?'

He didn't think she was, and it annoyed her intensely that he should be determined to provoke her this way. Why did he have to assume that she wasn't capable of putting in one hundred per cent? The man was a chauvinist.

'I'm not afraid of hard work,' she told him stiffly. It was true. It had been Colin who had objected to the hours she put in, and he'd had a point, because the hours she'd worked as a junior doctor in the hospital had been hellish. Still, she hadn't been the one to complain.

'Even so,' Martyn said, 'the hours might seem convenient to you now, but there may be times when extra help is needed—when we're short-staffed, for example. How would that fit in with your plans? You have a small son—are your child-care arrangements adequate to ensure that you'll be able to concentrate fully on your work?'

She lifted a finely arched brow. 'I hope that they'll be more than adequate to cover any eventuality, Dr Lancaster, though I'm afraid I can't give you an absolute guarantee that matters beyond my control will never upset them.' She paused, slanting him a cool green stare. 'Should these questions form any

part of the modern interview process? If I were a
man, I doubt you'd be putting them to me.'

'Hah!' John Stokes gave a short laugh. 'She's got
you there, man. Women's lib, you know, and the
feminist movement. Can't argue with that.'

'Can't I?' Martyn Lancaster scowled.

'I've had no complaints about my work so far,'
Sarah said. 'I can only tell you that I'll do my very
best for the practice.'

'You'd have to, if you were expecting to stay for
any length of time.'

The brusque dismissal scraped a raw edge along
her nerves. What had she done to make this man set
himself against her? Could it be that the eligible Dr
Lancaster hadn't enjoyed getting the cold shoulder?

John Stokes intervened. 'I believe Dr Lancaster
and I would like a few minutes to confer, Sarah,' he
said. 'I'll get my receptionist to show you around the
place, if you like, and then we'll bring you back in
here to let you know our decision.'

Sarah had little doubt what that decision would
be. Martyn had not made it easy for her, and she
was pretty certain she had done the wrong thing in
confronting him. He hadn't liked it, and if he was
one day to become the senior partner she had most
likely ruined any chance of being taken on here.

Looking around the building, she found it to be
well thought out, and extremely modern, with the
patients' comfort well to the fore. It was carpeted
throughout in a restful blue-grey cord, and the walls
were painted in a clean magnolia tint. There were

oil paintings—landscapes—mounted on the walls of the waiting-room, and there was a children's play area with neatly stored toys and a table for Lego construction.

Martyn came himself to find her and take her back to the office a short while later. She could read nothing from his expression, and took it as an ominous sign, so that when John Stokes said affably, 'Well, my dear, we'd like to offer you the job. What do you say? Will you take it?' she looked at him in stunned surprise. 'I hope you will,' he said. 'We were very impressed with your previous record and with the way you conducted yourself.'

'Thank you,' she managed, aware of a pair of glittering blue eyes turned her way. How much of this decision had been John Stokes's, she wondered, and how much Martyn Lancaster's? 'Of course I'm delighted to accept.'

'Good,' John said, sending her a beaming smile. 'We should celebrate. What will it be, coffee or something stronger?'

'Just coffee, thanks,' she murmured, still dazed by the news. 'I have to drive home.'

'So be it. When can you start? We'll be glad to have you with us. You'll find we're a happy, friendly bunch when you get to know us.'

He turned to deal with the coffee-maker in the corner of the room, and Sarah couldn't help a flickering glance in Martyn's direction. The ghost of a smile crossed his mouth as though he read her uneasy thoughts, but he said nothing, instead tugging his tie free of his collar and loosening the top button of his shirt. Sarah's gaze focused on the brown column of his throat, then she looked quickly away, her pulse beating a strangely accelerated rhythm.

She said huskily, 'I could start the week after next, if that's all right with you? It will give me time to tie up any loose ends.'

'That will be just fine,' John agreed, handing out cups of coffee. 'Help yourself to cream and sugar.' He sat down. 'Does your husband work locally?'

'My husband died two years ago,' Sarah told him, aware of Martyn's shifting away from the window.

'I'm sorry to hear that,' John said. 'That must make life difficult for you, with a young child to cope with alone.'

Sarah smiled faintly. 'We get by.'

'I'm sure you do. You look to me like a very capable person.'

They chatted for a while longer, then Sarah stood up to go.

'I'll see you out,' Martyn said.

They walked to the main doors, and she stopped to put on her coat, seeing that it was still raining. Martyn's fingers lightly grasped the collar, brushing the nape of her neck as he helped her on with it. A tingle of awareness trailed the length of her spine and she blinked, bemused by the unfamiliar sensation.

'Thanks, I can manage,' she murmured.

'Hands off—is that the message?' His mouth

twisted. 'Tell me, Sarah, is it just me that you have an aversion to, or do you already have an ongoing attachment?'

His glance flicked over her, and she was suddenly aware of her femininity in a way that was utterly disturbing. Working with him was going to be fraught with danger; she could see it coming.

'I have no aversion to you, Dr Lancaster,' she said, striving to keep a steady tone. 'I'm sure we shall be able to find some way of working together without constant friction. As to any attachment I might have, you can rest assured I won't let it interfere with the job.'

'I'm glad to hear it,' he said drily. 'You have yet to prove your worth, and I shall be watching you, every step of the way.'

CHAPTER THREE

ON HER first day in her new job, Sarah set out in good time, intending to reach the health centre at least an hour before morning surgery. She was full of optimism for the future, and her spirits were buoyant as she drove along, though she acknowledged a few minor qualms about how things might go on this very first morning. It would take her a while to get the feel of the place, and the patients were bound to be curious about her, the newcomer in their midst. She wondered what they would make of her.

Nothing was going to daunt her today, she vowed, not even the anxiety she had felt on leaving Daniel a short time ago, with his new nanny. The girl was going to take him to the nursery, and he should be happy enough there—it wasn't as though it was unfamiliar to him. Sarah had taken him there herself on several occasions recently to get him used to it. He'd been in a difficult mood, though, this morning, and it had taken all her reserves of patience to cajole him out of his sulks and coax him into smiles.

'I'll see you at lunchtime,' she'd said, 'and you can show me what you've been making at school.'

Things were bound to be difficult for him at first, but once he had made friends he would surely soon adjust to their new life.

Musing on this, she turned the car on to the riverside approach road, and felt a stab of dismay at the sight which met her. The waters of the river and the nearby locks must have been rising steadily over the last few days, because now the overflow had spilled on to the road, and several drivers were making slow progress attempting to get through.

She cut her speed to a crawl, wondering what to do for the best. The water must be about halfway up her wheels, and she wasn't sure that it would be a good idea to go on. Better to turn round and take another route, perhaps, only by now the traffic was building up behind her and it was going to be difficult to manoeuvre the car.

Just then, a lorry driver, tired of waiting, began to overtake, heading for the bridge over the river, and Sarah felt the swish of water as it buffeted the car when he went by. Her engine stalled, then died, and she listened to the silence in stark disbelief. She tried the ignition again, but nothing happened, and she gripped the steering-wheel, her fingers tight with frustration. Any delay with the car was bound to mean that she would be late arriving at the surgery, and that was too unsettling to contemplate. She could just imagine what Martyn Lancaster would have to say. She shook her head as though that might clear the image. This simply couldn't be happening to her. Not on her very first day. Anyone would think the fates were conspiring against her.

Reluctantly, she decided that there was only one thing to do, even if it meant getting out of the car and ruining her shoes in the flood waters. With a rueful grimace, she pushed open the door and climbed out. In future, she'd make sure she kept a pair of waterproof boots handy for emergencies like this.

A look under the bonnet didn't help. No matter what she tried, the car refused to start, and that didn't leave her a lot of choice as to the action she should take. Reaching for her car phone, she tapped in the number of the motoring organisation she belonged to, summoning help, and then, more hesitantly, put in a call to the centre.

'I might be a little late getting in this morning,' she said, struggling to keep the tension out of her voice. 'I'm stuck in the flood waters by the bridge, and I think my car is suffering from an overdose of damp. I'll be with you as soon as I possibly can.'

Other motorists helped to push her car out of the way, and she settled down to waiting, standing by a stone wall, miserably conscious of her ruined shoes and cold, wet legs. Checking her watch for the twentieth time, she reflected unhappily that all her good intentions to arrive bright and early were slipping away with every tick of the second hand. Martyn would probably be furious and she'd never hear the last of it.

Almost as though thinking about him had conjured him up, he appeared in the distance at practically the same moment as her mechanic knight errant and his overalled mate pulled up alongside her with their breakdown truck.

Martyn didn't make the same mistake as she had, but parked his gleaming silver Peugeot well back from the water. His mouth made a grim line as he approached her, and she swallowed hard, readying herself for the blast.

'I thought you said you were familiar with this area,' he bit out tersely.

'I am,' she agreed, adding with quiet defensiveness, 'But I'd forgotten quite how bad the floods can be around here. I was about to turn back, when the car stalled.'

'If you'd had any sense you wouldn't have driven so close in the first place.'

'I was doing perfectly well until some maniac rushed past me in a lorry and half drowned me,' she retorted, stiffly resentful. 'I suppose you never put a foot wrong? Everything in your life is orderly and regimented and wouldn't dare to upset your tidy schedule, would it?'

She regretted her childish outpouring as soon as she had made it, and Martyn merely looked at her with scornful distaste.

'I'll disregard those remarks,' he commented crisply, 'and put them down to an excess of disrupted hormones.'

'You would,' she said through compressed lips. 'It wouldn't occur to you that even a man could get himself into a situation like this and might be forgiven for being just a fraction uptight.'

The mechanic coughed politely, cutting her off before she could build up any more steam.

'Can't do anything here, I'm afraid. She'll have to be towed to the nearest garage.'

'But I haven't time to be towed,' Sarah groaned, her voice raw with frustration. 'I'm a doctor; I have to be in surgery in half an hour.'

Martyn's eyes slanted over the mechanic.

'You can see to it that it gets to the nearest garage, can't you?' he interposed thoughtfully. 'You've someone with you to help, so it shouldn't be necessary for Dr Prentiss to go along with you.'

'Well, I suppose we could do that. It isn't usual practice, but——'

'Good. Then that's settled. And perhaps you will arrange for the garage to ring Dr Prentiss at the surgery later this morning?' He reached into his pocket and drew out a card which he handed over. 'That's the number. The doctor and I will leave you to it.'

He took Sarah's arm in a firm grip and hurried her away from there, striding briskly towards his car.

'Slow down, can't you?' Sarah demanded breathlessly, struggling to keep up the pace he was setting. 'I know it's getting late and we have to hurry, but I'd sooner get by without a resuscitator if I can possibly manage it.'

He stopped long enough to throw her a black stare and she gulped in a lungful of air. A shiver passed through her as the bitter cold of the morning settled chillingly around her and the damp began to penetrate her bones.

'You're cold,' he said, and it sounded almost like

an accusation, as though he thought she couldn't even be trusted to dress adequately.

'I'm wet,' she informed him curtly, looking down at her stockinged legs. 'If I'd known I was going to be wading through flood waters, I'd have worn wellington boots.'

His hard glance flashed along the slender length of her shapely legs. She thought he was going to say something, because his whole body was still for a moment and his lips parted slightly, but then he shook his head and blinked and turned instead to unlock the passenger door and pull it open.

'Get in,' he ordered tersely. 'There's a blanket on the back seat. You can use it to dry off a little. I'll put the heater on. It shouldn't take too long to warm up.'

'Thank you.' She was grateful for his consideration, however grudgingly it might have been given. 'I'm sorry to have put you to so much trouble,' she said, settling back against the comfortably upholstered seat with a faint sigh of relief. 'I really didn't expect you to come to fetch me.'

'I was in Reception, sorting out my house calls, when you phoned. I have to do the rounds this morning, so I was coming out here anyway.' He set the car in motion and the warmth from the heater began slowly to envelop her.

'I see.' He hadn't made a special journey to help her out of her predicament and that should have eliminated any feelings of guilt she might have. She couldn't think, though, why the knowledge of that should make her feel so prickly and out of sorts.

He grimaced, throwing her a look which scanned her taut expression.

'I don't suppose you do. If I seem at all short-tempered, it's because I hate these wretched roads when the floods are out. It makes visiting the patients so much more difficult, since I have to take long and tedious detours to get anywhere at all. I'm only thankful none of the cases appears to be a real emergency this morning.'

'I can understand how annoying it must be for you,' she murmured. 'It's time-consuming and the patients must get fretful wondering when you're going to arrive.' She glanced out of the car window as he negotiated a small island in the road. 'I'll take a different route from home to the centre from now on. It'll be a couple of miles longer, but it will be better than running into problems.'

'Whereabouts do you live?'

'I bought a small house in Cosserton, just a few miles from where my parents live. I couldn't believe my luck when I found it. It's exactly what I wanted, and it's just the right size for me and Daniel, with a lovely garden front and back. He'll be able to play safely without my having to worry about him.'

'There are just the two of you, then? No one else lives with you?'

She didn't answer for a moment and he sent her an oblique glance, saying, 'Am I being too personal, too direct? I'm sorry; it's my way. If I want to know something, I usually ask.' He turned his attention back to the road ahead. 'I shouldn't have thought I was asking anything out of place. After all, you did say it was two years since you lost your husband. That's a long time. No matter what you felt for him, you're young and life does have a habit of going on, no matter how much we'd like it to stand still sometimes.'

'It doesn't seem that long to me, and I'm not looking for any kind of involvement. I have my work and my son, and they're enough for me.'

She had no inclination to form any kind of attachment with a man. It had been her experience that it was an undertaking fraught with trouble of one sort or another, and something she could well do without. Besides, it had been so long now since she had dated anyone, she was sure she would find it an awkward and nerve-racking experience.

'How long were you married?'

'Just under four years. We married soon after I qualified.'

'That wasn't much time to be together, was it?' There was a note of understanding and compassion in his voice, and when he asked, 'Had he been ill?' she marvelled at how calmly she was able to answer.

'No, not at all. Colin was always a very healthy man. His death was sudden, and it was a great shock, but I've managed to come to terms with it.' She drew in a deep breath. 'You're not married, are you?'

He accepted her change of course easily enough,

telling her, 'I'm not. Sometimes I think it might have been better, as far as the patients are concerned, if I had been.' He smiled briefly, but didn't enlarge on that. 'I was engaged once, but it didn't work out.'

They were pulling into the car park at the centre by this time, and Sarah thought twice about asking him any more. She wondered if his failed engagement had put him off the institution of marriage altogether, and had left him preferring the freedom of a bachelor existence.

Her shoes had dried out a little, thanks to the efficient heater, and she felt a lot more comfortable as she slid out of the car on to the tarmac drive.

'Thanks for the lift,' she said, and Martyn raised a hand in acknowledgement as he drove off.

Walking through to Reception, she saw that James Castlemaine, the fourth member of the practice's team, was ensconced in there, sipping coffee, while his wife, Sharon, chatted to John. Their two young boys were occupied at a table, drawing pictures on large sheets of white paper.

'So you're the new addition,' the dark-haired woman greeted her with a smile. 'I've been looking forward to meeting you, but now just as you've arrived I must dash off straight away and see that Christopher gets to school on time. I shall hate it when Alex starts next year. You have a little boy, don't you? Why don't you bring him over to play with my two sometime? We could have tea together if you like. Are you free this afternoon?'

'I am, yes,' Sarah said, warming to Sharon's

vivacious, bubbly personality, 'and I'd love to come over, but I'm not sure what's happening about my car. It's had to go into the garage this morning.'

'Ah, the floods. We've all been through it,' James said, his grey eyes warm and friendly. 'No problem. I'll drive you over there when we've finished here, and if it's still not ready I'll take you and Daniel over to our place.'

'That sounds fine. Thanks very much.'

Matters having been arranged to everyone's satisfaction, Sharon gathered up the children and went out, leaving Sarah to look round the busy office with interest.

John had seated himself at a desk and was stabbing at a computer keyboard, muttering under his breath.

'Are you having problems?' Sarah enquired gently.

'Wretched computers,' he pronounced irritably. 'More trouble than they're worth. I could never understand what was wrong with using pen and paper, but I suppose Martyn's right, and we have to move with the times. I let him talk me into getting the latest technology, and now I'm paying for it. Every time I look at the screen the cursor flickers at me as though it's criticising me for not working fast enough. . .and then there are the printers—noisy things.' He leaned back in his chair. 'I expect you're well used to all this new-fangled equipment?'

She grinned at him. ''Fraid so. I was brought up on it.'

'Hmmph.' Getting to his feet, he said, 'I'd better explain how we organise ourselves. I know we went through it briefly before, but if you're anything like me you'll want to go over it again. This is another brain-child of Martyn's, designed to make us more user-friendly.'

He went over to the reception window and pointed out the notepads which were laid out there in readiness. 'We have one doctor on call, while the other three operate a first come, first served system. The girls in Reception take names and make a list as the patients come into the centre. They can see whichever doctor they prefer, providing the morning's list isn't full. It usually turns out that there are about a dozen names on each pad. Then we have an appointments system for the afternoon and early evening, which we take on a rota basis. Saturday morning surgery is a short one, for emergencies only.'

'That seems fairly straightforward,' Sarah commented. A thought struck her as she glanced around. 'I'm starting just in time for the flu season. Do we have vaccine in stock?'

John nodded. 'We do. We took the precaution of ordering early, and we have enough supplies to cover all our most essential cases, the elderly or the chronically ill, and so on. Other patients who want a jab will ask at Reception, and we'll put them on our list and give them a date when they can see our practice nurse.'

The waiting-room had started to fill up with

people as they had been talking, and Sarah glanced down at the pad which had her name at its head. The list was growing rapidly, and she made her way to her room and prepared herself for her first patient of the morning. A few minutes later a young woman, slender and looking rather pale, seated herself in the leather-backed chair by her desk.

'I think I'm pregnant,' she said. 'I've had a test done at the chemist's shop on the corner, and the pharmacist gave me this form.'

It was indeed a confirmation of pregnancy, and Sarah glanced at the case-notes displayed on her computer monitor and asked, 'Do you know the first date of your last period, Mrs Markham. . .Catherine? And is your monthly cycle an average one, twenty-eight days?'

Catherine confirmed all the details that were needed, and Sarah asked her to lie on the couch so that she could gently examine her.

'I felt sure I was pregnant because my breasts have been feeling really strange,' the girl said. 'Tingling and heavy, and completely different from usual. And I've been running to the loo every five minutes.' The last was said with feeling, and Sarah smiled.

'Those are among the first signs,' she said. 'I'd say you were about eight weeks, which makes the baby due round about the end of May.'

Catherine's mouth curved, tilting in an expression of growing joy.

Sarah watched her, glad that her first diagnosis

here had been the beginning of a new life. It seemed like the perfect start to her new job.

'I'll arrange for you to see the midwife here at the centre, and the obstetrician at the General,' she told Catherine. 'We operate a shared care system, so you'll see one or other of us throughout your pregnancy. I'll see you every few weeks to begin with, then more frequently as your time gets closer. The midwife will want to take a blood test, and usually on each visit you'll be asked to give a urine sample.'

The girl groaned. 'I hate needles,' she said. 'I really hate them.'

Sarah gave a comforting smile. 'You'll probably find it's not nearly as bad as you think. Just a tiny prick, and over in seconds. The midwife will sort out all the details of appointments with you, and explain how our system works. She'll give you forms for prescriptions, dental care and so on, too.'

'Thanks, Doctor.'

Catherine left the room, leaving behind her a little of her warm glow of happiness, and Sarah pressed the button to signal that she was ready for the next patient.

He was a man in his mid-forties, of average height and lean build. He was coughing, the harsh, deep-seated cough of a bronchitic. Sarah glanced quickly at her screen as he sat down.

'Good morning, Mr Templeton. What can I do for you?'

'It's my chest again, Doctor. I think I need some antibiotics. It's been getting worse over the last week or so. I thought it would clear up on its own, but it hasn't done, and I'm beginning to feel really under the weather with it. I can't afford to keep having time off work.'

'If you'd like to take off your jacket and shirt,' Sarah said, 'I'll run the stethoscope over your chest.' He did as she suggested, and she went on, 'I see from your records that you suffer from bronchiectasis. How does that affect you generally?'

'The cough is there most of the time, but sometimes, like now, it's worse than others.'

'Do you attend the hospital as an outpatient?'

'Not any more. I used to have to go every year until I was around twenty, but then they discharged me and said I was to ask for antibiotics when things got stirred up again.'

'That would seem the sensible thing to do. And do you do any breathing and postural drainage exercises?'

He pulled a face as he began to dress. 'When I have time. I work shifts at the moment, and when I finish I'm either too tired or seem to have a thousand jobs to do round the house and garden. We've just built a new extension and I'm putting in the wiring for it.'

'You're an electrician, aren't you? Does your job affect your chest at all?'

'Sometimes, if I have to chop out walls for the cables. There can be a lot of brick dust.'

'I think you'd be well-advised to wear some kind of industrial mask when you have to do anything that creates dust of any kind,' Sarah said. 'And you really ought to try to make time to do your exercises, you know, even if it's only for ten minutes a day. Your chest is certainly congested, so I'll prescribe some amoxycillin for you, and I'd like you to come and see me again in a couple of weeks so that I can check that everything's cleared up.'

'Will do.'

'I think we might consider giving you a stand-by prescription to use in future as soon as you feel your symptoms coming on. There's no point in taking antibiotics simply for your cough, but when the lungs are congested and infection sets in you need something to clear it up quickly.'

She handed over the prescription, and as he stood up to go she added, 'I'd also like you to go and see Nurse before you leave. I see you haven't had a flu injection yet this year. Ask her to sort that out for you now.'

'I've been meaning to come in, but I didn't seem to get around to it.'

Sarah's eyes sparkled. 'There's no time like the present, Mr Templeton!'

She was kept so busy for the rest of the morning that it was almost a shock to find that it was nearly lunchtime, and that she was actually beginning to feel quite hungry. Her thoughts went to Daniel, and the favourite meal of beans on toast that she had promised him.

The garage had rung earlier to say that her car was fixed and ready for collection, and, with James offering her a lift, her morning was turning out to have been quite successful after all.

The phone rang as she was collecting up papers from her desk and pushing them into her bag.

'Sarah,' her mother said, 'I wanted to know how your first morning had gone.'

They chatted for a while, then Sarah, detecting a slightly strained note in Martha's voice, asked, 'Is anything wrong, Mum? It isn't Dad, is it?'

'I am worried about him,' she admitted. 'He's finally given in and told me that he's been seeing double these last few days. Do you have any idea what could be wrong? Could it be his retina detaching again?'

'I shouldn't have thought so. Is it affecting one eye, or both?' Sarah asked.

'Both, he says. What is it, do you know?'

Sarah bit her lip. If it was both eyes, then it could be that something was affecting the muscles that moved the eyes.

'It could be a number of things, Mum, but we shan't know until he has some tests. He must see the specialist. I'll come over this evening, shall I, and talk to both of you?'

'Would you? Oh, thanks, Sarah. That will make me feel so much better.'

Her mother rang off soon after that, and Sarah finished sorting through the bits and pieces on her desk, her mind filled with anxiety about her father. The sooner he saw a specialist the better, as far as she was concerned.

Still preoccupied, she left her room and went out into the corridor, colliding softly with a man's lean frame. James's hands went around her arms, steadying her as she stumbled backwards, and she stared up at him a little blankly.

'Are you OK?' he asked, his voice etched with concern. 'You walked right into me.'

She swiftly tried to collect her scattered wits. 'I'm fine, thanks. I'm sorry, my mind was miles away.'

'Problems with the morning's surgery?'

'No, everything went very well, I think. It was just that I had a phone call—my father is having some trouble with his eyes. He——'

'Still here?' Martyn addressed James crisply as he came along the corridor towards them. 'I thought you had calls to make.' His glance skated over Sarah, his expression cool.

James removed his hands from her shoulders. 'So I have,' he agreed amiably. 'I was on my way to the treatment-room to collect something when Sarah and I literally bumped into each other.' About to move away, he said as an afterthought, 'Is our game of squash still on for this evening? You've not made other arrangements?'

'I haven't,' Martyn answered.

'Good. Eight o'clock, then. Be prepared, I'm going to pay you back for last week.' James turned to Sarah. 'Do you play squash?'

She shook her head. 'It always looks far too energetic for me. Is that how you two let off steam?'

James nodded. 'You need something in this job to

help get rid of the tension. It keeps the muscles toned too.'

Sarah agreed. 'I'd rather swim,' she told him. 'I've been trying to introduce Daniel to the beginners' pool, and I think he's taking to it.'

'Sharon's looking forward to meeting him,' James said. 'I just have to get some bandages from the treatment-room, but I'll be ready to take you to the garage in ten minutes, if that's OK with you? I'm going that way, so it's no bother at all.'

'Thanks, I'll be ready.'

James went off along the corridor, leaving her alone with Martyn.

'It hasn't taken you long to wind everyone around your little finger, has it?' he said. 'I'd refrain from getting into clinches, though, if I were you. It doesn't look good to passers-by.'

'There are no passers-by,' she pointed out thinly. 'And it was an accident. I was preoccupied, and I simply wasn't looking where I was going. Excuse me, will you? I have to get my coat.'

Dismissively she started to walk away, and his hands shot out, capturing her arms and pulling her back towards him. His touch had a strange effect on her, a sensation of instant fire that raced through her bloodstream and left her feeling dazed and breathless. She stared up at him, bemused. The blue eyes returned her gaze steadily, and he said softly, 'As I said once before, you really will have to learn to keep your mind on the job, otherwise there's no knowing what predicaments you might find yourself in.' Then his mouth twisted into a mocking smile and he released her, moving briskly away.

She watched him go, her nervous system leaping and jerking in chaotic disorder. How on earth was she to work with this man? He was provoking and unsettling, and she didn't think she had ever met anyone quite like him before.

CHAPTER FOUR

OVER the next few days, Sarah did her best to make sure that her attitude towards Martyn Lancaster, at least outwardly, was purely professional. It wasn't easy. In the short time she'd known him he'd made a sharp and indelible impact on her senses that was thoroughly disturbing. She'd have liked to be able to distance herself from him, but that would have been impossible, meeting at the health centre every day as they did, and instead she tried to put up a calm, unaffected front, even though she was constantly aware of him in the background. On the occasions when she had to discuss anything with him she kept her tone cool and measured, determined not to allow herself to be provoked in any way. She didn't know yet what made him tick, but she was pretty sure that, where she was concerned, male chauvinism had a strong part to play.

His pronouncement on Thursday morning that he would accompany her on her rounds was typical, she thought, of his arrogant manner towards her.

'There's really no need for you to do that,' she said. 'I'm sure I shall manage perfectly well on my own.'

'It's more than likely you will, but a couple of new estates have been built since you were last hereabouts, and they can be confusing for newcomers trying to find their way around. It could take you twice as long to get through your list.'

His reasoning was sound enough, but it didn't stop her from feeling spiky at the thought of his coming along with her.

'But it will leave the surgery short-handed if you're with me,' she pointed out with what she hoped was faultless logic.

'That's no problem,' he countered briskly. 'John's wife has agreed to step in for me for the morning. She says it will ease her into retirement more gradually if she can fill in for one or other of us occasionally.'

He had everything covered, and there was nothing she could do but give in with as much grace as she could muster. The prospect of having him right by her side for the next few hours wasn't going down at all easily with her, and she felt sure he was well aware of that.

His gaze slanted over her, the blue eyes glimmering in a way that was thoroughly discomfiting. It made her pulse quicken and her heart begin to thud heavily against her ribcage. She dared not think what was happening to her blood-pressure.

'I hope you won't find the Metro too cramped,' she said, unlocking her car doors and making a brief assessment of his long legs through the curtain of her golden eyelashes. With half an ounce of luck he might still change his mind.

'I'll push the seat back,' he said with wry amusement as he slid into the seat beside her and strapped himself in. He studied her stiff profile with frank interest. 'You have to take ten out of ten for trying, but you must know things couldn't go on the way they have been between the two of us for the last few days.'

'I'm not sure that I understand what you're talking about,' she muttered as she started the engine and headed the car in the direction of the first address on her list.

'Let's not beat about the bush, Sarah. You know exactly what I mean. We have to work together whether you like it or not. You can't go on putting out prickles whenever I'm anywhere near you.'

'I wasn't aware that I had. I'm just trying to do my job the best way I can, knowing that you're constantly looking over my shoulder to see whether I'm doing it properly. It can be very trying, being constantly vetted.'

'Is that what I'm doing?' He looked genuinely surprised. 'I hadn't meant to give that impression. If I appeared to be watching you, it may have been that I was concerned to see that you were settling in all right. Some of the time, over these last few days, you've been a little withdrawn, as though you had things on your mind, and I shouldn't like to think that you were trying to cope with a problem entirely alone. You're part of a team now.'

'I know that,' Sarah said hurriedly. 'And thank you for your concern, but I think I've managed to feel my way through this first week, and everything seems to be falling into place fairly well.'

'You haven't come across any problems in surgery?'

'Nothing really. So far it's all been fairly routine. Several women have asked about the value or otherwise of hormone replacement therapy, and I'm finding that I don't have the time to go into it as fully as I'd like. I think we should stock up on leaflets, or advise them where to read up on the subject more fully. Other than that, I've no complaints about how things are going.'

He was studying her, his gaze sharply perceptive, so that she almost began to fidget.

'But something else is troubling you, I feel sure of it. And I don't believe it can be put down to any mere difference of opinion there might have been between you and me. Whatever's bothering you, you could do worse than to share it with us, you know. We're here to help. There's no point in struggling on your own when we could perhaps lend a helping hand to sort things out.'

Sarah drew in a quick breath. She hadn't expected such thoughtfulness from him, and perhaps that only went to show how little she really knew him. It was true that she'd had things on her mind lately, but she'd tried to keep them to herself, to keep her private life divorced from her work. She hadn't wanted to give Martyn the chance to say that she was letting her anxieties interfere with the job. Even now she was doubtful about confiding in him. He'd been against her from the outset, and how could she be sure that in telling him about her problems she wasn't loading him with ammunition to use at a later date? She wanted to appear competent and in control.

'I hadn't realised anyone had noticed. I may have been a little preoccupied just lately, I suppose. It's very kind of you to ask, but I'm fine, really.'

'No worries about your son—Daniel, isn't it?'

A little frown pulled at her brow. Concentrating on steering the car around a bend in the road, she said slowly, 'He's finding it hard to settle. There've been a few tantrums, mostly with his new nanny. I'm sure he likes her really, and he's just testing how far he can go with her, but it makes life difficult sometimes. We'll work it through, though, I'm sure. He enjoyed playing with Alex and Christopher when we went over there.'

Martyn seemed to accept her answer for the time being, and allowed their talk to revolve more around the work in hand as Sarah's time was taken up with her house calls. They were mostly routine visits, including a couple of cases of flu, and a patient recovering from a hip operation.

They were on their way back to the centre, passing by a small close made up of single-bedroomed bungalows, when Martyn said suddenly, 'Slow down a minute, will you? I think I saw something in a window just then.'

Sarah slowed, then backed up where he indicated and drove into the close, where she could see a red distress card precariously angled against the front window of one of the bungalows.

'What is that?' she asked. 'Some kind of call signal?'

'It's an idea we came up with to help some of our more elderly patients feel secure,' he told her as she pulled up in front of the bungalow. 'If they need help they put a card in the window so that neighbours or friends can see it. Something must be wrong. I'll see if I can find out what's happened.'

She got out of the car with him, following him along the path and peering through the bow-window as he rapped on the door.

There was no answer, and she said quietly, 'I think I can see someone, Martyn. On the floor by a bureau. Can we get in round the back?'

'I'll try. If the door isn't unlocked I'll have to force an entry through a window.'

A few moments later they were inside the house and kneeling beside its elderly occupant, a white-haired man who was obviously in great pain. He was pale, and beads of sweat had gathered on his forehead, but he was still conscious. He tried to speak, though it was an effort for him to get his breath, and Martyn said quickly, 'Don't try to talk, Jim, just show me, if you can, where the pain is.'

Jim's hand went shakily to the centre of his ribcage. 'Heavy,' he said. 'Arm as well.' His fingers wavered over his left arm, and Martyn nodded. He was busy loosening the man's collar and feeling for the pulse in his neck. Sarah produced her stethoscope, and he accepted it from her, moving it slowly over their patient's chest.

'It looks as though you've had a mild heart attack, Jim,' he said at last, 'but you'll be all right; we've got everything under control.'

Between them, he and Sarah drew Jim to a semi-recumbent position, then Sarah looked around the room and produced a couple of plump cushions to put at the man's back.

'That should help you to breathe more easily,' Sarah said. 'I'll go and call for an ambulance.'

There was a phone on the hall table, and she wondered if Jim had been making his way towards this when he had collapsed. At least he had managed to push the card against the window before the heart attack had worsened, otherwise it could have been some hours before he was found. She didn't like to think what the consequences of that delay might have been.

As soon as she had made the call, she went to look in the bedroom and pulled the duvet from the bed.

'The ambulance is on its way,' she said, going back into the room and kneeling to wrap the quilt around the man. He was in deep shock, cold and clammy to the touch. 'Is there a relative I can call, do you know?'

'He has a brother, Ted,' Martyn answered. 'I've seen him visiting sometimes. The number's probably by the phone.'

Jim nodded and said weakly, 'Lives in the next village. Barton.'

She went off to make a second call, relieved when she found that the brother was at home. Once again she returned to the living-room and passed on the message. 'Ted will make his way straight to the hospital, and he'll bring you anything you need as soon as you're settled. Don't worry about anything, Jim. It will all be taken care of.'

Relieved, Jim closed his eyes, relaxing just a fraction as the pain-killing injection Martyn administered began to do its work, and they stayed with him, quietly reassuring him, until the ambulance arrived a few minutes later. They supervised his transfer to the vehicle, then made their way back to Sarah's car.

'You're very quiet,' Martyn said as she turned on the ignition and pulled away, out of the close. 'I'm sure he'll be all right once he gets to the hospital. We found him in good time.'

'Yes. I was thinking about his brother, about how upsetting it is for the relatives to know that someone they care about is ill.'

'You're a doctor, Sarah. You're supposed to keep yourself detached as far as possible.'

'I know.' She tugged at the fullness of her lower lip with even white teeth. 'But if it happens to someone you love it isn't so easy. . .'

'Has it?'

She stared at him blankly for a moment before shifting her attention back to the road ahead, and he

said again, 'Has it happened to someone you love?
Your husband?'

She blinked, his words jerking her concentration
back into play. 'No. I wasn't thinking of Colin.' The
thought startled her for a moment, and she was
quiet, musing on the fact that she could so easily
dismiss her husband from her mind. It seemed such
a long time ago that he'd died, and even longer since
things had started to go wrong for them. She took in
a deep breath and, because Martyn was still waiting
for some kind of answer, said bleakly, 'I've been
worried about my father. He's been recovering from
an operation for a detached retina, but now there's
a new problem—some double vision that's getting
steadily worse.'

'Has he been referred for tests?'

'Yes, but I'd like to get things moving more
quickly—I've been making enquiries, but lists are
full and I want him to see the best.'

'Presumably the surgeon who saw him before
specialised in retinal work and lasers? This, of
course, might be something different.'

'Yes. That's what I'm afraid of.'

'Look, why don't I have a word with Nathan
Price-Jenkins? He's well-respected, and he owes me
a favour or two. I'll see if I can get him to take a
look at your father.'

'You know him?' Sarah felt her heart miss a beat
at the name she'd heard before, though usually it
had been whispered in almost hallowed tones. 'Oh,
would you? I'd be eternally grateful.' Her attention

was distracted momentarily by their arrival at the health centre, and she drew the car to a halt in the car park before turning to look at Martyn properly. 'I can't begin to tell you how relieved I'd be to have Mr Price-Jenkins agree to take on my father's case,' she said.

'Leave it with me.' He smiled, and she felt a peculiar melting sensation begin somewhere in the pit of her abdomen, as though all her bottled-up tension were being released in a slow stream of warm honey. It was the first time he had really smiled at her, and she drank in his expression, the mobile curve of his mouth, the faint lines that crinkled around his eyes. She felt a strange compulsion to reach up and touch his cheek with her fingertips, to cup his face in her hands.

Instead she said softly, 'Thank you.'

She had lunch with Daniel, then returned to the centre later in the afternoon to deal with her appointments. Catherine Markham was one of these, she saw, glancing through her paperwork and noting that the midwife had observed a considerable amount of sugar in the young woman's urine sample.

'It's nothing we need worry about at this stage, Catherine,' Sarah told the girl when she was seated in her room. 'This sometimes happens in pregnancy. But we need to keep an eye on things, and I think to begin with we'll take a look at your diet and see if we can deal with it from there.'

'I haven't felt like eating anything in the last few

mornings,' Catherine admitted. 'I've been feeling sick and dizzy.'

'You'd probably feel better if you could manage a cup of tea and perhaps a slice of dry toast before you try to cope with the day.' There was a dancing light in Sarah's green eyes. 'This is where your husband could come in handy.'

'Fat chance!' Catherine said with dry humour. 'I have to prod him to get him up and off to work every day as it is. All this talk you hear about the so-called New Man—where is he, that's what I'd like to know? If you ask me, it's a myth concocted and served up in magazine features.'

'A tea-maker, then,' laughed Sarah, reaching for the sphygmomanometer. 'I'll just check your blood-pressure.'

A few moments later she said, 'That's fine.' Taking two printed sheets from a folder, she handed them to the girl. 'This diet sheet gives advice on which foods you should avoid, and tells you which foods you can eat plenty of. I'd like you to follow it for a week, then come back into the surgery and we'll take another urine sample to see if there's any improvement. You must eat regularly, so be sure not to miss out any meals, but try to avoid any foods that have sugar in them. Things like chocolate biscuits, cakes, jams and so on. A lot of foods in the shops now are sugar-free; it's just a question of looking out for them.'

'Is it safe to use sweeteners in my tea?' Catherine asked. 'I'm thinking of the baby. I don't want it to come to any harm, and there's no way of knowing how long I'll need to cut out the sugar, is there? I've never used them long-term before.'

'There shouldn't be any problem with sweeteners. The general advice given to diabetics is to change the type they use from time to time. There are saccharin-based ones or Aspartame or Acesulfame K. You just need to check which brand is which.'

Mrs Markham left the room, busily scanning the information sheets as she went. From her wry expression, Sarah could see that some of the advice was going to prove hard to follow!

The afternoon passed quickly, and it seemed no time at all before Sarah's last patient of the day was being ushered in. From her records, she could see that the slim, dark-haired woman was in her late twenties. She had two young children with her, and looked vaguely harassed. She was also limping.

'I hurt my foot several weeks ago,' Mandy Simpson told her. 'Well, both feet hurt really, only one was worse than the other. I came to see Dr Stokes about it originally. Mrs Stokes, that is. She got one of the nurses to bind it up for me, and that helped a bit, but the pain didn't really go away. Then she gave me some tablets, and things were fine for a while, when I took them. I've finished all the tablets, though, and the pain has all come back.'

Sarah quickly read through her notes. 'You were out walking when you thought you hurt your feet? You said you might have twisted something, but both feet hurt after you'd been walking for a couple of hours, is that right?'

'Yes. They swelled up, and I couldn't wear my usual pair of shoes. My hands hurt now as well. It's causing me some problems at work—I'm a typist—just mornings, but I'm finding it hard because my fingers are so stiff and painful. My shoulders, too.'

Sarah nodded understandingly. 'I think I should examine you, Mandy. Would you like to take off your coat and sit on the couch? Perhaps the children could stay with our receptionist for a few minutes. She'll find them some toys to play with.'

'Would she mind?' Mrs Simpson asked. 'I've just collected them from school.'

'Of course not. I'll take them along to her.'

Sarah examined the woman carefully, noticing the swollen and inflamed joints in both hands.

'Are your fingers stiff all the time?' she asked. 'Or do you notice any changes through the day?'

'They're always worse in the morning, first thing,' Mandy said. 'It takes me a while to get started these days, with getting the children ready for school and trying to get breakfast. Everything takes me longer than it used to because it hurts to do little things like turn on the tap or lift the kettle.'

'That would make life difficult,' Sarah sympathised. 'Come and sit by the desk again, Mrs Simpson.'

Mandy Simpson dressed and sat opposite Sarah once more. 'Will I be able to have some more of the tablets that Mrs Stokes gave me? They seemed to help take away the pain in my feet.'

'Yes,' Sarah said. 'I can certainly give you some of those. But I think we need to look into your condition a bit further, Mrs Simpson, and I'd like to arrange for you to see a doctor at the hospital. If I put you on his list now, you shouldn't have to wait more than a few weeks to see him. He'll want to ask you a few questions, and possibly do blood tests and take a sample of your water. He may want to do X-rays, too.'

'What kind of doctor? Is it something serious?' Mandy looked worried, and Sarah hastened to reassure her.

'He's a consultant rheumatologist, and he's an excellent doctor. I think you may have a form of arthritis, but we shan't know until certain tests have been done, and then we'll be able to look at your case again and decide on more specific treatments.'

'Arthritis?' Mandy echoed. 'But I thought that only happened to old people. I'm only twenty-eight.'

'Unfortunately it can affect both young and old. But it needn't be something to upset yourself about. These days there are a lot of things we can do for people with your problem, and the sooner we make an exact diagnosis, the sooner we can start dealing with it effectively. In the meantime, I think you should consider taking a couple of weeks off work to rest those fingers. Exercise is good in moderation, but while your joints are swollen and stiff like this the best thing would be to give them a break from the typing.'

'Yes, I suppose you're right.' Mandy looked pale

and abstracted. 'I don't know how I shall cope if they stay like this. Typing's my job. It's what I'm trained to do.'

'Let's see how you get on over the next few weeks, shall we?' Sarah advised softly. 'The anti-inflammatory tablets that I'm prescribing are very good at giving relief, as you found before.' She tore the prescription form from the printer and handed it to Mandy with a smile. 'Your appointment should come through within three or four weeks, and we'll take it from there. In the meantime, if you have any problems, come back and see me.'

Mandy Simpson went to collect her children, and Sarah sat back in her chair, feeling suddenly drained. She hated this aspect of her job, this feeling of acute helplessness. None of her training had shown her how to overcome the frustration and despair she experienced whenever she had to break bad news to a patient. She always hoped it would get easier as time went by, but it never did.

Her fingernails dug into the palms of her hands as she fought the wave of unhappy thoughts that threatened to swamp her. Life was so unfair, disease so cruelly indiscriminate. . .

'Am I interrupting anything? You couldn't have heard my knock at the door.'

Sarah looked up to see Martyn standing in front of her desk, his tall frame blotting out everything else. She stared at him, resenting the intrusion, her breathing laboured as she tried to master her emotions.

'I didn't.'

'I saw that your last patient was leaving so I guessed you'd be alone. What's wrong?'

'Nothing's wrong. What should be wrong?' she said tautly, holding herself severely in check. 'Did you want me for something?'

'Tell me,' he persisted. 'Stop bottling it all up.'

'What's to tell?' she said. 'I'm just doing my job, the same as we're all doing, day after day, trying to heal the sick. Isn't that what we're about?' She stared at him, her eyes faintly shimmering, her face set with anger and wretchedness rolled into one. 'Sometimes I wonder if we know anything at all—if we're not still locked in the Dark Ages.'

Her jaw clenched, her mouth making a grim, hard line, and Martyn watched her, waiting.

'Go on,' he urged. 'Is this something to do with the patient I just saw leaving?'

'She's only twenty-eight years old. Twenty-eight. Just a year younger than me, and she has all the signs of rheumatoid arthritis. She has a young family to cope with, a job. It makes me so angry, so frustrated when I see what cards some people are dealt.'

'It happens,' he said. 'You see it every day, so there's little point in getting yourself into an emotional state about it.'

'How can you be so calm?' she asked restively. 'Don't you ever get angry, feel like railing at the world?'

'It would do me precious little good if I did. We

do what we can to relieve suffering, and medicine has come a long way in the last few years. Even in the treatment of arthritis. You know that. There's a lot we can do to help. Besides, there's hope that this new genetically based treatment will work wonders.'

'Maybe it will, but the clinical trials could take years before it's accepted. In the meantime Mandy has to cope with the disease. It seems so unfair.'

'Life *is* unfair. Your patient's situation could have been worse—she might have been afflicted by a life-threatening illness; but she wasn't.'

Sarah stood up, her mouth stiffening. 'Is that supposed to make me feel better? I wish you would stop being so reasonable about everything. You've obviously never bothered to envisage what life is like for someone with that condition, otherwise you wouldn't——'

'And you're jumping to conclusions, talking like an overwrought, over-emotional female.' Sarah opened her mouth to object again, and he said firmly, 'I know very well what the illness means to the people who suffer from it. My own grandmother has had it for years. She's the reason I went into medicine in the first place, because she was an inspiration to me. Still is, in fact.' He looked at her, his features harsh, unsmiling. 'As for you, Sarah, you've got to toughen up if you want to survive in this job. It isn't like any other, and you can't take on the grief of the world. We do what we can, we do our best, and our knowledge is growing all the time. That's something we can take heart in, something to pin our hopes on. Your patient is going to get the best of medical care, and her chances of living a normal life far outweigh those that my grandmother had.'

'Yes.' Sarah said the word on a breathy little sigh. 'I know that. It was just—seeing her with the children, seeing the apprehension that came into her eyes when she thought about her job and how she might be affected—it all just hit me smack in the face.' She straightened her shoulders. 'Tell me about your grandmother. How does she cope?'

The corners of Martyn's mouth lifted in a faint smile. 'She's bright as a button. She has the occasional off-day, usually when she's been a little too adventurous in the days before and done more than she should have. Most of the time, though, she's chirpy and cheerful, and fiercely independent. My parents wanted her to go with them to live by the coast, but she wouldn't have it. She was determined that she wasn't going to spend her days in a granny annexe when she could stay put in her own little house, surrounded by her friends. Of course, she visits my mother and father, and they come to see her regularly, because it's a relatively short drive from the coast to the Midlands.'

'She lives near here?'

'Yes. At least I'm here to keep an eye on her. I don't believe my parents would have moved house if that hadn't been the case. And they know that she's sensible. She listens to advice and follows it, and she's careful about her medication. It means that

she's free from pain most of the time and she's able
to keep herself active.'

'Do you have any other family?'

'A brother, but he's away most of the time. He
works as a Reuters correspondent, so we have to
make do with the occasional flying visit, or a post-
card every now and again.' He ran a finger along the
smooth, polished wood of the desk. 'What about
you? Any brothers or sisters?'

She shook her head. 'No one. Only my parents,
and Daniel.' She thought about them, a faint smile
touching her lips before it was tinged with sadness.

Martyn said, 'You're worried about your father,
and that's understandable, but you shouldn't let your
anxiety colour your attitude to your work. You can't
afford to be emotional, but you're definitely uptight,
and it's no wonder, with a small son to care for as
well as all the other demands made on you. You
need to unwind a little.'

'I'm all right.'

'You're not, but I think I may have a cure. Let
me take you out one evening, for a meal or to the
theatre perhaps. It might do you the world of good
to relax. From what I've heard you don't have much
of a social life outside work.'

Sarah stiffened. 'Am I to take it that I'm the focus
of everyone's conversation these days? I hadn't
realised that everything I said was going to be
bandied about and dissected.'

'It wasn't like that, believe me. Just a casual

remark that I happened to overhear. What's your answer, Sarah? Do we have a date?'

She thought carefully before answering. 'It's a nice idea,' she said slowly, 'and it's very kind of you to offer to cheer me up. But, as you said, I haven't been used to much of a social life, and I don't think I'm quite ready for dating yet. I really think it would be better if we kept things between us on a purely professional footing. That way we both know where we stand, and there's no danger of any misunderstandings.' She sent him a quick, darting glance. 'I hope that doesn't offend you. I'd like us to be friends.'

His eyes were cool, narrowed on her.

'Do you know what you are, Sarah Prentiss?' he said tersely. 'You're a coward. First, last, and every way there is. A coward.'

CHAPTER FIVE

MARTYN'S words rankled with Sarah throughout the following days. She wasn't a coward, she told herself repeatedly. She was cautious, that was all. If you'd made one bad mistake in your life, you weren't going to rush whole-heartedly into making another one, were you?

Not that a simple, no-strings date with Martyn Lancaster would have led anywhere at all, of course. That was all in the realms of supposition and imagination. . .wasn't it? Her mind veered sharply away. She simply wasn't taking any chances. She'd learned to be wary, that was all, and she wasn't about to take a leap in the dark after all this time, no matter how cynically he viewed her reaction to him.

Besides, she had Daniel to consider. He wasn't used to seeing her going out and about with men, and those he did see her talking to he viewed with suspicion. There was a lot going on inside Daniel's little head, because despite his tender years he was bright as a button. She had yet to find a way of getting him to talk about his insecurities, and the whole area of her relationships in the meantime was fraught with tension. Sooner or later she must deal with the situation, she knew that well enough, but for the moment she tried to concentrate on giving him as much of her attention as she possibly could.

'I want to see where you work, Mummy,' he had said one day, and she didn't see any reason why he shouldn't pay a visit with her to the centre on Saturday morning. They weren't usually busy after eleven, and she wasn't on duty this weekend.

'Bring him in by all means,' John Stokes said. 'The boy can have a look around. I'll be clearing up a backlog of computer work in my office, so he won't be disturbing anything, and Martyn will have finished his surgery by then, I expect.'

Sarah looked forward to the extra time she could spend with Daniel at the weekends. She was with him for a good portion of most afternoons, and he should have been much more settled by now, but if she had one worry it was that he was still being difficult with his new nanny. The girl was calm and understanding, though, heavens above, Daniel could try the patience of a saint at times, but even she was becoming anxious about his obstructive behaviour. Somehow Sarah didn't think it could only be put down to simple attention-seeking.

On Saturday, though, he was in high spirits, chattering brightly to Sarah and to his teddy bear throughout the journey to the centre. As soon as they arrived, they went through to Reception, and she was glad to find that he was content to sit and draw while she quickly scanned her post, and checked up on the smattering of patients' notes that had been updated by the clerk yesterday afternoon.

Catherine Markham's latest urine test, she saw, had again shown a rather large quantity of sugar. Frowning, she reached for a notepad and left a message for the receptionist to contact the girl on Monday morning. She would need to come in sometime during the week for a glucose tolerance test, a GTT, so that they could establish whether there was a possibility of gestational diabetes. It could well be that she was simply one of those women whose renal threshold was such that an excess of sugar spilled over during pregnancy without causing any problem, but they had to find out for certain.

Catherine wasn't likely to take kindly to the test, Sarah thought with a faintly rueful smile, considering her aversion to needles. She'd have a glucose drink first of all, and then three lots of blood would need to be taken within the space of a couple of hours to see how her system coped with it. Once Sarah had spoken to the girl and explained things, she'd talk to the practice nurse and make the necessary arrangements.

'I've had enough of drawing, Mummy,' Daniel announced, coming to wave a large sheet of paper in front of her face. 'I've done a picture of you, and a picture of Benjy and me. Look.'

Sarah studied the colourful drawing of huge potato-shaped characters with spindly arms and legs, and gave him a quick hug.

'That's wonderful, sweetheart. You've even given me a red skirt, just like the one I'm wearing, and a jumper too.'

'Benjy hasn't got any clothes,' Daniel said, fixing her with a hard look. 'He's cold.'

'Oh, dear. Well, he still has some fur left to keep him warm.' Sarah put the notes she had been making into the receptionist's tray and said cheerfully, 'Shall we go and see if we can find Dr Stokes?'

They walked along the corridor in time to see Martyn coming out of his room. Daniel stopped, legs firmly braced, and he clutched Benjy tightly to his chest. He stared up at the man who towered above him, and Martyn greeted him with a smile.

'Hello, young man,' he said, bending his knees and coming to rest on his heels beside him. 'I've seen you before, but I don't think I met this fellow.' He stroked the teddy bear's silky golden ear with the tip of his finger. 'As I recall, you were in too much of a hurry for us to be introduced. What's his name?'

'Benjy.' Daniel's lower lip jutted out. 'But he's not very happy, so he won't talk to you.'

'Oh?' Martyn lifted a dark brow. 'Why's that?'

'He's cold, 'cos Mummy didn't make his jacket yet.'

'Ah.' Martyn nodded sagely, shooting an oblique glance in Sarah's direction. 'Too busy, hmm?'

Sarah screwed her face into an expression that was wryly penitent.

'I *have* had a lot to do just lately,' she said in her own defence, 'but there's only the button band left to knit. If I get the time, I'll try to finish it this afternoon.'

Daniel thought that over, and appeared to find the answer acceptable.

'What have you got in there?' he said, standing in the doorway of Martyn's room and peering around.

'Shall we go in and take a look?' Martyn laid an encouraging hand on the boy's shoulder and together they went inside. Sarah followed, going over to the window where the slatted blind let in the cool autumn sunlight.

'It's a zoo!' Daniel exclaimed in delight, his wide-eyed gaze drinking in the selection of colourful stuffed toys that lined the shelves, and floated down from the ceiling on bright strings.

'So it is.' Martyn smiled. 'I think my favourite's the giraffe. You can play with him if you like.'

Tempted and curious, Daniel reached for the soft toy Martyn held out to him. He gave a little chuckle as his fingers curled into the felt, though he made sure that Benjy was still held tightly in the crook of his other arm.

'Benjy wants to say hello.' Within minutes, the two animals were holding their own peculiar conversation, and Martyn, seeing that the boy was engrossed, took the chance to draw Sarah to one side. He was no longer smiling, and Sarah quickly scanned his expression, noting the faint, almost imperceptible line that had etched its way between his black brows.

'You've heard something,' she said. 'About my father's tests?'

He nodded. 'Nathan has the results,' he told

her, keeping his voice low so that Daniel wouldn't hear.

A trickle of ice ran down her spine, and there was a catch in her voice as she asked, 'What has he found?'

Martyn grimaced. 'He's eliminated any possibility of diabetes, hyperthyroidism and vascular disease.'

'And the CAT scan?' Sarah's mouth was dry. 'What did that show?'

'There was something, Sarah, but of course it may be quite innocent. It looks as though there's a small tumour present, and that means he'll need to operate. He'd like to do that as soon as possible. Do you think your father will agree to it?'

'Yes. I'm sure he will after I talk to him.' Her stomach muscles had clenched in rigid denial of the news she hadn't wanted to hear, and for a fleeting moment she almost swayed. Martyn's hands came at once to grasp her elbows, firm and supportive.

'It may not be anything serious, he said gently. 'It could well be benign.'

'I was dreading this,' she said huskily. 'All along, I was afraid of something like this.'

Just then, John Stokes approached the room, and Daniel wandered to the door, holding up the giraffe for him to see.

'He's hungry,' he said. 'His neck's so big it takes him too long to fill his tummy up.'

'Then we'd better see what we can do about it,' John said, glancing at Sarah's strained expression and making a swift interpretation. 'Come along to my room and I'll put my thinking cap on.'

'What's a thinking cap?' Daniel wanted to know. He trotted along the corridor after John, and Sarah watched him disappear around the corner, staring after him, unseeing.

Martyn closed the door. 'It might not be anything to worry about, Sarah,' he said. 'Either way, we could know within a few days. Nathan's a skilled surgeon; he'll make sure that everything's done that should be done. Try to stay calm.'

'I don't feel calm.' Her mouth was taut, her fingers twisting restlessly. 'I feel angry and bitter, and I want to know why this should happen. I feel so useless.'

'You've done all you can for the moment. Try to put it to the back of your mind until we know more.'

'How can I do that? It's easy for you to say, isn't it?' Her voice rose slightly, a betraying tremor in the words. 'It's my father we're talking about.'

Martyn's hands shifted to curve around her shoulders. 'I know that. I do know what you're going through.'

'You don't know, you can't know——'

'Why can't I?' His jaw was hard, controlled, only a flicker of muscle giving any sign of his own inner tension. 'Because you believe I'm too cold, too unfeeling to know what normal human emotions are all about? Isn't that what you think?'

She drew in a shaky breath, knowing that she wasn't being fair to him. She was being every bit the

over-emotional female that he was so contemptuous
of.

'This isn't your problem,' she managed. 'I owe
you so much already for helping me, for arranging
everything, but now I must deal with this by myself,
in my own way. There's no need for you to be
involved.'

She tried to pull away from him, wanting to be
alone, to think, to come to terms with what she had
learned, but he didn't let her go. Instead he drew
her towards him, his hand moving behind her head
to capture the slender column of her neck and tangle
in the silky mass of hair at her nape. 'Perhaps I want
to be involved. I'm human enough, Sarah. I feel
too. I care. Perhaps it's time you realised that.'

He sounded quietly angry. The words were forced
out in a roughened undertone and, hearing it, she
looked up at him, her eyes widening, focusing with
renewed clarity on his tautly honed features, on the
firmly moulded mouth that hovered just inches
above her own. She was held fast within the circle of
his arms, her soft curves crushed against his hard
frame, so that she could almost feel the tension
vibrating within his long, muscled body.

'You don't have to be alone in this,' he muttered.
'There's no reason for you to barricade yourself
inside that damned wall of ice and shut everyone out
the way you do.'

'I didn't mean to do that,' she said shakily. 'These
last few years I've learned to be self-sufficient. I've
had to be; I don't know any other way.'

Martyn sighed, bending his head towards her, his hand shifting slowly over her spine and pressing her gently into the heat of his body. 'Come in from the cold, Sarah,' he urged softly.

The husky tones lapped at the edges of her resistance, while all the time his touch stirred her dormant senses to a growing, tingling awareness. Looking up at him, she knew that he was going to kiss her, and it hazily registered on her shell-shocked mind that she ought at least make one last effort to escape. . .

She didn't move. Her limbs were strangely weak, and instead she clung to him, her fingers curving over his wide shoulders, taking the support they offered. She felt oddly out of synch with everything around her. Had her lips really parted in traitorous expectation? she asked herself as his head slowly bent towards her. She ought to have pulled away; even now she could have made some attempt to drag herself back from the brink before it was too late.

Moments later she was lost to all thought as his mouth closed on hers, and began to explore the softness of her lips with a warm and tender possession that was unexpectedly sweet. It took her by surprise, that coaxing embrace, stealing the breath from her.

She was lost to all reason as the kiss deepened in intensity. Her body seemed to have a will of its own, her soft, feminine contours moulded to his hard-muscled frame as though the two were made to complement each other, meeting in supple, aching need.

The depth of her body's response shocked her. Had she ever felt like this before? She didn't think she'd ever known such instant, mind-shattering awareness as this and it brought a shimmer of bewilderment to her eyes, made her stare up at him in uncertain dismay.

His own eyes reflected the battle that was going on inside her. Tension sparked in the blue depths, a glittering, febrile emotion flickering there, and she saw it and recognised it for what it was. Desire. Nothing more, nothing less. She saw it at last, and that above all else pulled her to her senses, bringing all her defence mechanisms surging to the fore.

He had started off with good intentions, she was sure, offering her comfort, and it was her own fault that she had been weak enough to accept it, grateful for a fleeting gesture of friendship that might warm her aching heart. She had no one to blame but herself for what had happened next.

She made a last, belated effort to draw away from him, a new and unaccustomed ache growing inside her, and as the door slammed back against the wall behind them Martyn let her go. He looked. . . stunned. . .as though he had woken from a dream and found his hands engulfed in flame.

Daniel marched into the room, oblivious for once of the vibes disturbing the air around him.

'We got enough Smarties to fill giraffe's neck,' he announced. 'Dr Stokes keeps them in a big jar in his cupboard. Only I had to eat them, 'cos giraffe wouldn't open his mouth. He wasn't hungry at all, not really. He was just p'tending. I like it here. Can I come again?'

Martyn's jaw flicked spasmodically, his mouth making a grim line, and Sarah swallowed, struggling to find her voice.

'I should think so,' she managed. 'If you're very good, and if Dr Stokes doesn't mind.'

'He doesn't,' Daniel said with conviction, turning to look at the large desk now that the matter was settled to his satisfaction. 'What's in there?'

He was looking at an ornately carved, polished wooden box, and Sarah searched for some way to distract him so that they could both leave before they outstayed their welcome. Martyn raked a hand through the gleaming jet of his hair.

'My special pen,' he supplied, and his voice was so deep and even that Sarah felt an irrational resentment that he should have recovered himself so quickly and adapted himself to Daniel's eager questioning with such ease. 'Open the box and have a look inside.'

Daniel did as he suggested, and was clearly impressed by the sight of the slim gold pen that nestled on a bed of dark velvet.

'Why's it speshul?' he asked.

'It was a gift,' Martyn said, 'a present,' and Sarah was stricken by a peculiar pang in her mid-section as she wondered who had bought it for him. It was no secret that he could have had any number of women friends. Her gaze met his across the top of Daniel's fair head, and he added with quiet pride, 'My parents gave it to me when I qualified as a doctor.' Turning his attention back to Daniel, he went on, 'I use it for my prescriptions, when I've decided what medicine will make my patients feel better.'

Daniel shook his head vigorously. 'Dr Stokes says you print 'scriptions on the 'puter,' he contradicted in the tone of one who knew better. Chin lifting, he waited for Martyn's response.

Martyn smiled. 'So I do. But when the prescription has been printed I use this pen to sign my name, and sometimes, if the computer isn't working properly, or if I'm making house calls, I write the whole thing out.' He gave the teddy bear a searching glance. 'I think Benjy could do with a prescription, don't you? Something to keep out the cold.'

He tore a blank sheet from his pad, and wrote swiftly across the white form before handing it to Daniel.

'There you are. For Benjy Prentiss, one knitted jacket, to be worn every day. Signed Dr Lancaster.'

Daniel's mouth cracked into a wide smile, and he promptly wafted the paper gleefully in front of Benjy's face. Martyn joined him in studying the teddy bear's reaction, and Sarah, watching the two males, heads almost touching, felt an odd twist in the region of her heart.

She was being overly sentimental, she told herself. Daniel had no father, and Martyn. . .well, Martyn was turning out to be not at all what she had first imagined.

She was beginning to like him, perhaps a little too much for her own well-being, and she ought to have known better than to let her feelings run away with her.

He was just a man, she reminded herself firmly, a man who, with typical male arrogance, had made a play for her. He didn't need any encouragement; he was just practising what he had been doing since he was old enough to leave his mother's apron strings, and he'd have no hesitation in taking any opportunity that presented itself.

She ought to have learned her lesson by now. There were few men who could be relied on, men that you could put your trust in, and she would have to be a prize fool to let herself in for that kind of hurt again.

Besides, he was a colleague, and she had to work with him, hopefully for longer than just a few months. It would be the height of folly to jeopardise her job here at the centre by getting involved in any way other than professionally. She definitely couldn't afford any entanglement with Martyn Lancaster.

'It's time we were going home, Daniel,' she said, and even to her own ears the words sounded sharp. Martyn glanced at her, then straightened up, his tall presence making the room seem suddenly very much smaller.

'Want to stay,' Daniel complained, but Martyn placed a hand on the boy's shoulder.

'Better do as your mother says, Daniel,' he

remarked quietly. 'It looks as though she's in a hurry to get away.'

Sarah took her son's hand and walked to the door, conscious the whole time of a dark and brooding stare fixed on her as she made her escape.

CHAPTER SIX

WINTER must definitely be on its way, Sarah decided some days later. She could feel the nip of ice in the air as she made her way to her car in the dark, early hours of the morning. Her breath froze in a little white cloud as she scraped the windscreen and she wryly acknowledged that this was one aspect of the job that she most certainly did not like. Getting up from a warm bed to go out on a call was not something she'd recommend to anybody.

Not that she'd been asleep. Too many things had been plaguing her mind for her to be able to rest properly. Knowing that her father would be going into hospital tomorrow—today, she corrected herself with a yawn as she slid into the car and peered at the digital clock, was bound to leave her feeling edgy with worry. His operation was scheduled for the following morning, and, although she knew that Nathan Price-Jenkins was thought to be the best surgeon for miles around, the knowledge only in part eased her anxieties.

Her father had reacted better than she had.

'I may as well go in and get it over with,' he'd said quietly. 'At least it'll serve to put your mother's mind at rest, knowing we'll soon be told what's what.'

Sarah had hugged him, but she'd felt cold inside, as though the season that was fast descending around them had insidiously crept into her bones.

It bothered her, too, that she'd had to leave Daniel with her mother tonight. Daniel's nanny had announced suddenly, three days ago, that she had been offered a job abroad and had to go right away. The announcement had come like a bombshell, and even now Sarah was reeling from the shock of it. It had overturned all her careful arrangements, but perhaps she should have seen it coming. She'd known Daniel could be hard to handle at times, and he'd never fully accepted the girl, but she'd hoped that they would at least have had a little longer to get used to each other.

Martha had stepped in. 'I'll look after him for you until you can sort something else out,' she'd insisted despite Sarah's protestations. 'It'll be no trouble at all. I love having him around the place and he likes being with us. He'll be company for me while your dad's in hospital.'

Sarah knew full well that her mother was already burdened with troubles of her own, and she hated having to add to them. What choice did she have, though? The girl's defection had left her with a major problem to deal with, and she had to resolve the situation fast because, however willing she was, Martha certainly couldn't be expected to cope, not now. And Martyn would be sure to have something to say if Sarah's domestic arrangements got in the way of her work schedule. He'd made his views on that score plain enough at the interview and she didn't think it likely that he would have had a change of heart.

That kiss had changed nothing. In fact, the tentative bond which had until then been slowly growing between them seemed to have withered away completely. It seemed as though he regretted what had happened and had withdrawn from any close contact with her. For the last few days he had been treating her with nothing more than cool formality and she was bewildered by the range of emotions that behaviour stirred in her. She'd thought it was what she wanted, but now she wasn't so sure.

At least they managed to work together without undue friction, and all she could really do was to try to keep things running as smoothly as possible.

Stifling another yawn, Sarah turned her thoughts to the job in hand, stopping the car outside Mrs Benson's bungalow on the outskirts of the village. Cautiously manoeuvring herself along the path, shrouded in darkness, she went to rap on the front door.

'Oh, it's you, Doctor,' Mrs Benson said, looking strained and pale. She managed a weak smile. 'You're the one who helped me when I fell and hurt my ankle near the health centre, aren't you? I'm so glad to see you again; you were so kind to me that day. Come in, please. Don't stand out in the cold.'

Following the old lady as she walked into the compact front room, Sarah took the chintz-covered armchair that was proffered and asked gently, 'What

exactly is the problem, Mrs Benson? When you
phoned you were a little vague. You mentioned that
you were in pain—that your ankle is troubling you.'

Margaret Benson's lower lip quivered slightly
before she managed to bring it under control. 'I. . .
Yes—well, I thought it was throbbing a bit. That
must be it.' She frowned distractedly. 'I couldn't
sleep, you see, and I thought. . .though it's not too
bad, you know. I'm getting about the house all
right.'

'I'll take a look, shall I?'

Sarah took a few minutes to examine the ankle
carefully, then returned to sit down, a small frown-
line working its way across her normally smooth
brow. It was very perplexing, because everything
seemed to be healing nicely, and Mrs Benson had
shown no outward signs of any pain when Sarah had
gently manipulated the joint. The swelling had gone
completely, and there had been nothing at all that
might have given her cause for concern.

'Have you been taking pain-killers?' she asked.

'Not so many, now, these past few days,' the
woman admitted. Her voice lowered, drifting as she
turned to gaze into the soft glow of the gas fire. 'It's
been a lot better. I haven't really needed them.'

Sarah studied the bent grey head thoughtfully.
'Has your neighbour been in to look after you? You
said you thought she might.'

'She's been very good,' Margaret said quickly.
'She came in every day, twice a day at first. Of
course, she's very busy. She works part-time, down

at the factory on the industrial estate. I couldn't expect her to keep coming around now that I'm so much better.'

'So it isn't really the ankle that's giving you trouble?' Sarah queried.

'Well I. . . I thought it was, really I did. . . I just kept tossing and turning, and I was feeling out of sorts and odd, somehow. I didn't feel right, if you know what I mean. I can't think what it was, but I'm not feeling too bad now, just a few aches and pains, and a bit of a cough. I shouldn't have called you out, on a night like this, too.'

The old lady looked thoroughly miserable and downcast, and Sarah commiserated quietly, 'Things always seem worse when it's the middle of the night and it's cold and dark outside, don't they?' Unlocking her briefcase, she drew out her stethoscope and said, 'I'll just take a listen to your chest and generally check you over, take your blood-pressure and so on.'

A few minutes later, she placed her equipment carefully back inside the case.

'Generally, I don't think there's anything to worry about, Mrs Benson. Your temperature's up just a little, and there's a bit of a wheeze in your chest, but we can soon clear that up with an antibiotic.' Her patient still looked unhappy and there was a faint shimmer about her eyes that caused Sarah to add, 'Have you been out of the house at all lately?'

'Not for. . .a week or so, I suppose it must be now.' The pale mouth quivered again. 'It's such a walk to get to the shops, and this cold weather takes my breath away, you know. It's icy too, and I'm afraid to risk the pavements.'

'We are having a mix of bad weather just lately, aren't we?' Sarah agreed. 'I think if you keep out of the cold wind for a few days more you should soon be feeling much better. You know,' she added, 'when you're feeling more like your old self again, I'm sure some of the local organisations could arrange transport for you so that you could get out and about. Do you belong to the Evergreens?'

Margaret shook her head. 'I never joined them. I'm on my own, you see, and I expect they're all couples, and they all know each other. I'd be a bit out of it. I don't know all that many people. I only came to live here a couple of years ago—well, the other place was too big after Harry died.' Her voice faltered and she looked away. 'We got on so well together, just the two of us. We were in that house for more than fifteen years, and I stayed on as long as I could, but in the end it was too much for me to manage on my own.'

'It must have been a wrench, having to leave it behind,' Sarah murmured. 'But perhaps the time has come for you to make more of a life for yourself here. I really think it might do you good to get out and about a little more and mix with other people. You wouldn't need to feel out of it at all, because I'm quite sure you'll be made to feel welcome in the local groups. From what I've heard, they have some lively meetings, coffee mornings, a whist drive and so on. . . . In the summer they hired a coach and went off on trips to the seaside. I could put you in touch with the organisers, if you like, and sort out arrangements for you to go along to some of their get-togethers. What do you say? Shall I do that for you? It wouldn't hurt to give them a try, would it?'

'I suppose not,' Mrs Benson agreed a trifle hesitantly. 'If you think it's a good idea. But I wouldn't want to be a trouble to anyone.'

'Heavens, they'd be only too happy to have you join them. Leave it with me, Margaret, and I'll see to it that someone contacts you in the next day or so. In the meantime——' Sarah drew her prescription pad towards her and began to write '—I'll drop this in at the pharmacy tomorrow morning on my way to work. Do you think your neighbour might be persuaded to pick it up for you?'

Margaret nodded slowly. 'I'm sure she will, if I give her a call. She goes into the village every day.'

'That's settled, then.' Sarah stood up and prepared to go. 'No, don't see me out,' she said as Margaret started towards the door. 'I can manage. Why don't you make yourself a warm, milky drink, and see if that will help you to get off to sleep? I expect you'll feel much better in the light of day.'

Reassurance and a human presence were probably a far better cure for what ailed Margaret Benson than any antibiotic could ever be, Sarah reflected as she made her way back to the car. She sometimes wished her own problems could be so easily solved.

There was still time to snatch a few hours' sleep

before she needed to put in an appearance at the centre, and she drove back to the cottage hoping that there would be no more calls that night.

She was out of luck. Before she even reached home, the soft trill of the mobile phone led her to change direction and head for the opposite end of the village.

Her patient, she discovered, had been suffering from a violent bout of vomiting and diarrhoea and was in severe distress. After hearing that he had been out earlier in the day and eaten a meal of chicken and chips and salad with egg mayonnaise, she strongly suspected that he was the victim of a salmonella infection, but only laboratory tests would prove that.

Notifying the appropriate departments took quite a while, and it was some considerable time before she finally returned to her bed. Exhausted, she pulled the quilt around herself and closed her eyes.

The irritatingly cheerful sound of the radio alarm woke her just as she was settling into a deep sleep. Dragging herself out of bed once more, she made herself eat a quick breakfast, then set off on the journey to her parents' house so that she could see Daniel off to nursery school.

When she finally did show her face at the centre, rather later than usual, she was feeling far from refreshed, and it didn't help matters to find Martyn already there, full of sharply focused energy, grimly contemplating his morning surgery list.

His glance skimmed her as she walked into the reception office, his expression darkly frowning.

'Good morning,' she said, shrugging out of her coat and sliding it on to a hanger.

'Is it?' The laconic tone made her pause slightly as she lifted the hanger on to its waiting hook.

'I certainly hope it will turn out that way,' she murmured, wondering what had brought on his black mood, and deciding to ignore it. 'I've been out on call most of the night, and though my body might be here my brain is still back home in bed. At least I don't have a surgery this morning.'

'That's just as well,' he remarked, a cool grimace twisting his mouth, 'because you might find you need the odd spare hour to make an extra journey sometime this morning.'

A look of puzzlement crossed her face, and he went on, 'Perhaps you haven't noticed that you're missing something? Your handbag? The nursery just rang to say you left if there when you dropped Daniel off a few minutes ago. Of course, it may not matter that much. Depends whether you just use it to store your sandwiches for the day.'

Sarah groaned, grimacing at her folly in leaving the wretched thing behind, but he hadn't finished yet. 'Doesn't say a lot for your concentration this morning, does it?' he pressed on. 'I thought you employed a nanny to deal with all the domestic hassle when you're supposed to be at work?'

'I did. She left.' The note of impatient censure in his voice made her prickle all over and she sent him a look of cold dislike. 'Besides, most of the time I prefer to take him myself if I can possibly manage it. He's my son,' she added pithily, 'and I don't regard him as "domestic hassle". As to my concentration, I have a lot on my mind at the moment, coupled with a broken night, so I dare say it's hardly surprising if I'm not functioning on all four cylinders.' Her brows drew together as she went over the events of the morning in her mind. 'I seem to remember putting my bag down on a table while I stopped a youngster from jumping up and down on a bench in the cloakroom. He almost banged his face on the coat pegs. . .and then Daniel produced his PE bag and said his vest had gone missing. . .along with a plimsoll. . .' Her mouth shaped her annoyance. 'I really don't know why I'm bothering to explain all this. If you're going through a particularly bad morning, perhaps you should deal with the causes of it, rather than spend time taking pot-shots at me over my concentration. I'm only here at all this morning to drop in on a patient having a glucose tolerance test, and to find out whether any more house calls have been rung in.'

Shooting him a frowning glance, she saw the muscle that flicked tightly in his jaw and wondered once more what had brought on his unaccustomed black mood. She couldn't be held responsible for it, surely?

His own glance moved glitteringly over her, making a swift assessment of the soft cashmere sweater that clung gently to her feminine curves, and slanting down to sweep over the neatly tailored skirt that emphasised the slender shapeliness of her legs. She had chosen her clothes carefully this morning, aiming to look cool and in control, but under that raking glance she felt her colour beginning to rise.

Crisply, she said, 'I don't like being used as the butt for your irritability.'

'Is that what I'm doing? Taking my temper out on you? I hadn't thought about it that way.'

'You are.' Returning his stare, she allowed her gaze to run the length of him from top to toe, taking in the clean lines of his dark grey suit, and the crisp finish to his pale blue shirt. His hair was immaculate, as usual, gleaming like jet in the rays from the overhead light, and there was a devilish attractiveness about him that brought an odd lump to her throat. She swallowed hard. She wouldn't let his hard-boned good looks sway her. It was one thing to try to keep the peace, quite another to let him walk all over her. She had the feeling that that was what he'd like to do right now, given half a chance.

'You're right,' he said. 'I am having a difficult morning.' He began to move restlessly about the room, pulling jerkily at the knot in his tie. 'As soon as I arrived here there was a rep waiting on the doorstep, fully expecting to be allowed an interview. No appointment. On his way to Oxford later, he said, and this would only take ten minutes, save him having to double back later.'

Martyn scowled, and Sarah almost found it in her to pity the obviously new and untried rep. 'I expect you put him right about that,' she said with a wry half-smile.

'I most certainly did. Told him where he could go and what he could do with his free samples. I won't be pushed into using products that I'm not happy with, which is what he was trying to do, and I absolutely refuse to start a discussion on them at eight in the morning before I've even had a cup of coffee. He went off with a flea in his ear.'

'I doubt we'll be seeing him again, then.' Sarah's glance went to the coffee-percolator at the far side of the room. 'Do I take it you've still not had coffee?'

'Not yet. By the time I'd got rid of him I had to sort out some files for my clinic later this morning. Some notes I needed to check up on. A new case referred to us a couple of weeks ago.'

'It's your morning at the hospital? I'd forgotten.' She went to pour two coffees while he skimmed the list of waiting patients. He nodded absently, and she queried softly, 'Is it a difficult case?'

'Hmm?' He placed the list back on the counter and looked up. 'Difficult? Not exactly. A child. Club foot. He'll need surgery. Never easy to explain these things to parents.'

Sarah could see now why he had appeared so tense when she had walked into the office. Clearly she wasn't the only one who found there were things about this job that were distinctly unpleasant.

He picked up his coffee and walked towards the

door. 'I'd better make a start on these, otherwise I'll still be here by lunchtime.'

'You don't usually take surgery on your clinic morning.'

'No. But there's been a change-around at the hospital. Staffing problems, while we're opening up a new wing, so we're starting at ten-thirty. And it means I can help out here a bit, because apparently James has been delayed this morning and will be in later than usual.'

Keeping busy, she thought. Keeping his mind occupied. At the door he stopped and turned to glance at her. 'You said you had things on your mind. What things? Daniel? Your father?'

'Both,' Sarah admitted. 'I thought I had all my child-care arrangements carefully worked out, and now they've fallen through. The nanny I was employing to look after him in the hours he's at home when I'm not around has gone off after pastures new. I really thought Tracy was beginning to settle with him, but it looks as though her patience ran out. Either that, or she had a yen to travel. Her new placement is in Switzerland.'

'Lucky for some,' Martyn commented drily.

'And unlucky for me. My mother has stepped into the breach temporarily, but with Dad going into hospital this afternoon she won't be able to keep that up. She'll have far too much on her mind.'

'You could try asking James's wife if she'd like to take him on. She's fretting about the time when both her boys are at school for the whole day, and she'd probably enjoy having him. He gets on well with Alex and Christopher, so that would be a bonus.'

Sarah turned over the idea in her mind. 'But Sharon used to be a nurse, didn't she? Won't she be ready to go back to work once the boys are off her hands?'

'From what James says, she doesn't appear to be in any hurry to do that, and when she does it will be on a part-time basis, maybe working for the health centre in some capacity. You could do worse than ask her.'

'Yes, it's something to think about,' Sarah said musingly, then added with a sigh, 'but Daniel's not an easy child to handle. There have been a lot of changes in his life, and he can be demanding and fractious, and——'

'Just ask her,' Martyn said. 'Why put obstacles in the way of something that could turn out to be a great solution?' He reached for the door-handle. 'Are you going with your parents to the hospital? To see your father settled on to the ward?'

'Yes. I've rearranged my appointments for this afternoon so that I can do that.'

Martyn nodded, unsmiling. 'You'll know soon enough what the score is.'

He pulled open the door and walked abruptly out of Reception. In a moment or two a buzzer rang, and the receptionist called for the first patient to go along to his room. Sarah gave a little sigh and went over to the desk to check up on her calls.

'Thank goodness he's in a better mood now,' the

receptionist said in a low mutter. 'No one's been able to put a foot right since he walked in here this morning. He used to frighten me to death,' she confided. 'But that was when I first came here. I'm more used to him and his ways now. I can't help thinking it's a good thing he isn't married, though. Any wife of his would need the patience of a saint.' She mused on that thought for a while. 'Then again, perhaps marriage would mellow him a little. . . I wonder. . .?'

'I shouldn't think there's much likelihood of that happening in the near future,' Sarah swiftly disabused her of the idea as she jotted an address down on her notepad.

'You're probably right. He was engaged once, but things went wrong and he's never been deeply involved since then.' The girl grinned impishly. 'He always ran too fast to get caught again.'

Sarah managed a faint smile, but the girl's words echoed her own thoughts almost exactly.

Turning her mind back to work, she said in a more businesslike fashion, 'Would you get through to Age Concern for me sometime this morning, and the Evergreens?' Briefly, she outlined Mrs Benson's situation while the receptionist reached for a pad and made some notes. 'Perhaps you could contact the mobile library service too, while you're about it.'

'I'll get on to it,' the girl said. 'She's a nice old thing, Mrs Benson. Very quiet, though, and always far too withdrawn into herself for her own good. Leave it with me, and I'll see they look after her.'

'Thanks.'

Checking her watch with the clock on the wall, Sarah went along the corridor to the treatment-room, where she guessed that Catherine Markham would any time now be having the second of her three blood tests of the morning.

The young woman, instead of being seated on one of the cushioned chairs in the secondary waiting-room, as Sarah had expected to find her, was lying down on the treatment-room couch. On the cork noticeboard opposite there were a few brightly coloured drawings sent in from the local primary school. They all bore the label 'Dracula', and most of them featured a man with a huge grin and exceptionally large, pointed teeth.

'Is everything all right? Are you feeling OK?' Sarah took note of the girl's pale features.

'I just felt a bit faint,' Catherine said. 'I had to lie down for a while.'

Sarah's glance went to the nurse, busy preparing a cup of tea for her patient.

'It was the sight of the needle that did it,' the older woman supplied, brown eyes sparkling. 'Went a delicate shade of green, she did!'

'That was nothing to that awful drink they gave me,' Catherine retorted. 'Pure sugar, it was. And they made me drain every drop. Yuck. I can still taste it now, more than half an hour later. At least the blood test was over and done with in a few seconds.'

'Well, my dear,' said the nurse, 'now that you've had your second blood sample taken, we can allow you a cup of tea. Only one more small syringe to fill and then you're done. You'll be able to go home and forget about it. Are you feeling a bit brighter now?'

'A bit. Thanks.' She sat up carefully and took the cup that the nurse handed to her. 'I need this.'

'Stay there for a while longer,' Sarah said, 'until the nurse thinks you're back to normal. We should get the results through sometime next week, so if you come into the surgery to see me then we'll be able to decide what needs to be done, if anything.'

'I will,' Catherine promised.

Sarah went out of the room, stopping to scan the leaflets on the rack in the waiting area. A few sheets of information on hormone replacement therapy caught her eye and she spent a few minutes studying them until she saw Martyn open the door to his room.

'Could I have a quick word before you see your next patient?' she asked.

'About what? I was just about to get an information sheet from the office.' He didn't look any too pleased at the prospect of being delayed, but it was too late for her to start having second thoughts now.

'About the information we supply to our menopausal patients,' she told him. 'I mentioned to you before that I've been getting quite a lot of queries about HRT and I feel that the patients are entitled to know more about what's involved.'

'And?'

She took in a quick, sharp breath at his impatient tone. This was the wrong time to ask him anything, and in the days to come she'd probably regret the fact that she hadn't chosen her moment more carefully.

'I was thinking of setting up a meeting one evening, inviting women to come along and hear someone speak to them about the subject. A consultant, perhaps, from the hospital. It could be a fairly leisurely affair, and they would have a chance to ask questions. It shouldn't be too costly to organise, and we could probably hire the local village hall for the occasion. What do you think?'

'Sounds like a good idea to me.' Sarah barely had time to be astonished by his swift agreement, before he went on, 'One that could be extended to other areas of medicine, if there were a demand. I take it you've already spoken to John about it?'

'Yes. He said to talk to you, since you'll be the senior man in a few weeks.'

'Put some feelers out, find out how much interest there is, and then you can go ahead and arrange it.' He started towards the office once more, then stopped suddenly and threw her a sharp glance. 'You look surprised,' he said. 'What did you expect me to say?'

Sarah gave him a faint smile. 'I'm not sure. I

wasn't convinced this was the right time to approach you. But then, you've been quite remote over the last few days, and now seemed as good a time as any.'

'Remote?' His mouth made a wry curve. 'That's a word that's open to interpretation. I was trying to keep things on a strictly professional basis between us because I thought that was the way you wanted it. Did I get the message wrong?'

Sarah's mouth dropped open as she thought about what she should reply to that, and he went on thoughtfully, 'I rather get the feeling you're a little confused about what it is you *do* want. It's probably down to the chaotic turn of events your life's undergoing just lately. Once you get those sorted out, you might be able to see things more clearly, and maybe then we can begin to make some headway.'

What he meant by that last remark she had no idea. 'I'm managing perfectly well,' she returned uneasily. 'I don't see any——'

'The plain fact is,' he cut in, 'you're too tense for your own good. You worry about Daniel because you think he's having trouble adjusting. You think his nanny left because of his bad behaviour and you blame yourself for that, when in all probability he's no better and no worse that any other boy of his age. You can hardly blame yourself for the loss of his father, and anyway he seemed to me to be well enough adjusted when I saw him last week. I can't see any reason why you should rack yourself with guilt over being a working mother. You owe it to yourself to follow a career if that's what will make you a fulfilled individual. Daniel will be all the better for it if you stay true to yourself.'

Sarah stared at him in wide-eyed, open-mouthed astonishment. He had recognised her fears and outlined the bare bones when she had scarcely even voiced them to herself, let alone the world in general.

Martyn's fingers lifted to cup her chin. 'Close your mouth,' he said, his voice rough around the edges, 'unless you'd like me to kiss it again.'

She closed her mouth promptly, gulping in a swift, sharp breath, and he said drily, 'See what I mean? Tense, uptight, and thoroughly keyed up. What you need is to wind down and forget your troubles for a while. . .and I have something in mind that will help you do just that. A little pre-Christmas get-together at my house, and you have no excuse whatever for not coming along. All the staff from the centre are invited, and there'll be a number of my colleagues from the hospital.'

'But I can't possibly,' Sarah began. 'My father——'

'Will expect you to go on living your life. If he's well enough, your parents can come too. And before you say it, I've a spare room where Daniel can sleep. I'm warning you now, Sarah, if you don't put in an appearance of your own free will, I shall come and fetch you myself.'

His thumb gently grazed the line of her jaw. 'Now

we've settled that little matter satisfactorily,' he murmured, 'I'd better get on with the rest of my surgery. I have to leave here by ten if I'm to get to the hospital in time for my clinic.'

'Satisfactorily?' she echoed. Were all males so steadfastly assured of their own superiority in making decisions? 'In whose opinion? Certainly not mine——'

She broke off as he planted a warm kiss firmly on to her soft mouth, and she felt the tingle of it reverberate right through her down to her toes.

'Must go,' he said, a smile crooking his mouth, and her skin heated as though he'd flicked a switch and let her have the full force of ten kilowatts. 'We'll talk over the arrangements later.'

He moved away from her and, dazedly, she stared after him, a strange melting sensation coursing through her limbs and leaving her feeling oddly helpless.

CHAPTER SEVEN

SARAH didn't think there was any way she could possibly get out of going to Martyn's party, and she was most definitely not looking forward to it. It seemed as though it had been such a long time since she had mixed on a social level—since Colin's death she had not thought beyond keeping body and soul together—and the fact that she now had to make some kind of effort gave her a feeling almost akin to apprehension. Everyone else was full of excitement about it, though, the talk in the centre revolving cheerfully around the coming event until she felt like blocking up her ears with cotton wool.

Her nerves were on edge, of course. He had been perfectly right about that, and it was mainly the worry over her father that was causing it. She had seen him on the day of the operation, and he had looked so frail and somehow intensely vulnerable, swathed in bandages, that she had felt the prickle of tears sting her eyelids and it had taken a real effort not to break down.

Even now, here at the hospital once more, when she could see through the glass panel of the side-ward's door that he was looking much more like his old self, with more colour in his cheeks, she had to blink to keep the waterworks at bay.

Martyn's hand gently squeezed her shoulder. 'I'll wait for you here in the corridor. Chin up. You've managed to put a brave face on things so far.'

She gulped on a half-hearted smile, and felt a sudden rush of warmth start up in her as she looked at him. 'It was really kind of you to offer to drive me and my mother here. You were right in what you said—I am too agitated to get behind a wheel today. It's odd, isn't it? I'm a doctor, I see this sort of thing every week, every month, and it hardly affects me, yet right this moment I feel completely and utterly churned up inside.'

'It's natural that you should feel like that. But at least you won't have to stay in suspense for much longer. Nathan's talking to your parents right now, and he must be telling them what he found. Why don't you go in there? It looks as though he's about through.'

She nodded, moving towards the door just as it opened and Nathan Price-Jenkins came out. She could read nothing from his expression, and as she went into the room she heard him behind her, greeting Martyn.

'Dad?' Sarah put her arms around her father and held him close. 'How are you feeling?'

'I'm fine, Sarah,' he said huskily. 'I'm fine.'

She looked at him, and then at her mother. Martha dabbed at her eyes with a handkerchief and then blew her nose fiercely.

'He is,' she said simply, in a choked voice. 'Mr Price-Jenkins said it wasn't malignant. There's nothing to worry about, and his sight should return to normal. All he's got to think about now is growing his hair back in time for Christmas.'

'Oh, Mum! Dad!' Sarah felt tears of happiness trickle down her cheeks, and she didn't care at all as she hugged each of them in turn. 'Isn't that the best Christmas present of all? I'm so happy, I could dance a jig!'

'Save that for my party,' Martyn said, appearing at her side, and smiling across at Richard. 'Good news, then? I'm really glad for you. Nathan had to rush off to another appointment, but he told me everything was a hundred per cent OK. I must say you look ten times better than you did yesterday.'

'Thanks. I feel it. What's this about a party?'

'My house, in a couple of weeks. If you're well enough by then, you might like to come along. Sarah's under orders, so she'll be there, of course, and you and Martha will be very welcome.'

Sarah sent a quick, narrow-eyed glance in his direction, and Richard laughed. 'It's about time someone took her in hand, and made her join in with things a bit more. She deserves to have some fun.' He looked across at Martha. 'I'm not sure about us, though. Depends how much my hair has grown by then. I shouldn't like to stand out like a skinhead.'

'And it depends on whether you're fully on the road to recovery,' Martha put in firmly. 'I want you fit and well for the Christmas celebrations, my lad.

Perhaps we'd better give it a miss. Besides, these young things won't want us around.'

'Not true,' Martyn said. 'But whatever you decide I hope there'll be lots of other occasions when we can meet up. I'm glad that I've had the chance to meet you both at last. Now all I have to do is to persuade Sarah to let her hair down a little. That shouldn't be too difficult now that she knows you're going to be all right.'

Sarah wasn't so sure that it would be quite that easy. As the Saturday of the party drew nearer she began to get more and more twitchy, not least over what she was to wear. Nothing vaguely party-like in her wardrobe appealed, and she decided it must be because of all the associations they bore with her time with Colin. Mostly she recalled hours of watching him flirt with other women, and though, on those occasions, she had never been short of male attention herself, the hurt had cut deep inside her.

The time had come, she made up her mind, to splash out on something new. A trip to town and the festively decked-out boutiques took up several hours and left her footsore and considerably short in the pocket, but in the end, surveying the things she had bought, she thought that perhaps it had been worth it.

The dress she had picked out was cut in folds that draped themselves lovingly around her slender figure and swirled about her calves as she walked. In delicate shades of sea-green, it highlighted the

colour of her eyes and, she hoped, did something to
enhance the creamy tones of her skin.

Zipping herself into it on Saturday evening, she
looked at herself carefully in the mirror, and began
to experience a new fluttering of anxiety. Had she
made a mistake in buying it? She wasn't sure there
ought to be quite so much bareness about the
shoulders—but perhaps her thin gold locket would
serve to distract the eye. Slipping matching gold
earrings into her pierced lobes, she slid her feet into
new shoes that matched the tones of her dress
exactly.

A quick spray of Rive Gauche, a present from her
parents, and she was almost ready. She searched for
her bag, touching up her lipstick and checking the
pins in her upswept hair, until a glance at her watch,
and Sharon's knock at the door, told her that she
could delay no longer.

'Are you ready, Daniel? We must go now. Alex
and Christopher will be waiting in the car.'

Martyn's house was just a couple of miles away
from the health centre, set back off the road, and
well-lit, so that they had no difficulty negotiating the
gravelled drive. It was a wide, L-shaped building
with dormer bedrooms that overlooked a well-
tended shrubbery at the front, and, she noticed later,
a long, sloping garden at the back.

Martyn took them through to the large kitchen
and offered them drinks—squash for the children
and a choice of wines, spirits and liqueurs for the
women. The kitchen was sumptuously set out with

oak units and an island bar with a hob and beaten-copper cowling. Sarah could only guess at the range of equipment in there, but she saw a discreetly hidden dishwasher when he drew out fresh glasses, and the fridge was stocked to the brim. He took out a jug of orange juice topped with slices of fruit and slid it on to the worktop.

'I've hired an entertainer for the children,' he said. 'Magician, cartoon show, that sort of thing. Send them through to the sitting-room and he'll see that they have a good time. Later, if they get tired, they can sleep in one of the rooms upstairs.'

'It was very thoughtful of you to do that,' Sarah said a few minutes later, when the children were happily settled. Sharon and James went off to talk to a couple of friends they glimpsed in the study, and Martyn ushered her into the lounge.

'My pleasure,' he murmured. 'I want you to relax and have a good time.' His gaze moved slowly over her, and she almost held her breath, wondering whether she ought to have worn something else, until he added softly, 'You look beautiful, Sarah.'

Her skin warmed under his heated, lingering glance and she said on a flustered note, 'Th-thank you. I. . . Your home is lovely, Martyn. It's warm and inviting. Everything is so perfect and. . .cared for. What I could see of the garden looked intriguing.'

'If it looks cared for, that's all down to my housekeeper. I'm hopelessly undomesticated,' he said, conceding her change of subject. 'I do like this place, especially in the summer, and I'm glad I decided to buy a couple of years ago. The garden at the back slopes down to the river, so it had to be carefully landscaped, with a couple of terraced lawns to make it easier to work. It took some doing, but it was well worth the hard work in the end.'

Sarah wondered if he had done the work himself. She looked at his large, capable hands, and thought that he probably had. It would have been a labour of love.

He smiled at her. 'I sit out there sometimes and feed the ducks as they come swimming by. I'm hoping one day they'll breed in the reed shelter—if they do, you'll have to bring Daniel along to see them.'

'He'd love that,' John Stokes put in, coming to join them. 'There's nothing I like better than to come and sit out by the river with Martyn on a peaceful summer's afternoon. . .unless I'm down by the lake fishing, that is. Or with the wife, pottering about in our garden.'

'Is that what you'll be doing after Christmas, when you retire?' Martyn asked. 'Perhaps we should get you a greenhouse as a retirement gift? You've always said you'd like to grow hothouse plants.'

'Freesias and exotics. . .capsicums. . .perhaps even the odd vine or two. Sounds good, doesn't it? Yes, I think I might like that.' John grinned. 'And if I didn't feel like working on anything, I could always sit in there and listen to Pavarotti and do *The Times* crossword, couldn't I? Always sends me to sleep, does *The Times* crossword. . .'

'I can imagine. Excuse me, will you both?' Martyn said, glancing around at the chattering crowd that was gathering in the lounge. 'I think some of my guests need to know where the buffet's set out.'

Sarah stayed to talk to John and his wife for a while longer before going into the room where the children could be heard laughing raucously. She watched the entertainment with them until Sharon joined her and they decided that it was time to take their sleepy offspring upstairs to bed.

'I'm glad you asked me about looking after him for you,' Sharon whispered some half an hour later as they crept out of the room. 'I shall have time on my hands soon, and there's nothing I'd like better than to have him with me. He's a bright little bundle, isn't he?'

They went down the stairs and into the lounge, where the lights had been dimmed and soft music was drifting from a pair of speakers on the far side of the room. Couples were dancing slowly, swaying together in time to the music, and Sarah saw Martyn in the midst of them, his arms around a brunette who looked as though she couldn't get enough of him.

'They were engaged once,' Sharon said, following the direction of her gaze.

'It looks as though they're still close,' Sarah remarked, trying to keep her tone light and even, and wondering why her breath should snag so in her

throat. The girl moved sinuously against him, and
Martyn laughed softly at something that she whispered in his ear. Watching, Sarah felt the fierce stab
of needles moving in unison down her spine.

'Maybe,' Sharon agreed. 'I was never really sure
what caused them to break up. He seemed besotted
with Louise and they always looked so good
together. Both dark and attractive, and they always
seemed to have a lot of fun, what with parties,
dinners, trips to the theatre and so on.' She glanced
around. 'Oh, there's Mike Brandon. I think you'll
want to meet him, Sarah. Didn't you say you wanted
to set up a meeting about hormone replacement
therapy some time? Well, he's your man. He's a
consultant at the hospital. I'm sure if you ask him
nicely he'll consider giving a talk for you and your
ladies. Jenny's with him. You remember her from
your stint as a locum in Casualty, don't you? She'll
introduce you.'

Sarah did her best to drag her attention away from
the absorbed couple on the makeshift dance-floor,
and tried to concentrate on what Sharon was saying.
Why should it bother her that Martyn chose to glue
himself to that dazzlingly lovely girl, who looked as
though she might have modelled for some exotic
beachwear catalogue, with her perfect figure and her
flawless honey-gold skin? She wouldn't pay them
any attention—she would ignore the pair of them.

Jenny was only too pleased to make the introduc-
tions, and when she was left alone with him Sarah
found that Mike Brandon was surprisingly easy to

talk to. He had a warm sense of humour and a sharp intelligence that shone through, and gave her some inkling as to how he'd make it as a consultant by his late thirties.

He looked remarkably young, with dark brown hair sweeping back from a smooth, high brow. His eyes were a curious mixture of brown and green, and they were thoughtfully focused on her as he said, 'A talk? I don't see any reason why not. The more women are better informed about HRT, the more readily they can make their choices. How many people did you say were interested?'

'I've had more than sixty replies to my questionnaire,' she told him, adding hurriedly, 'Though that's not to say that they would all turn up on the night. I thought I'd hire the village hall for the occasion. It's very good of you to agree to give your time like this.'

'I'm glad to. In the long run it makes my job simpler. I believe in keeping the public up to date with current thinking. They've a right to know what their options are. Let my secretary know what dates would suit you, and we'll see if we can come to an arrangement that pleases us both.' He smiled down at her. 'Would you like to dance? I'm not brilliant at this, but I can just about manage a slow shuffle.'

She laughed. 'I'd love to.'

For the next twenty minutes or so, Sarah gave herself up to the rhythm of the music, and found to her surprise that she was actually enjoying herself. Mike had lied about his prowess as a dancer, and she was able to fit her steps to his so that they were soon moving together with an easy familiarity. He swung her around as the fast disco beat faded to a conclusion, his hand resting lightly on her hip, and she looked at him and smiled widely.

'I haven't danced like that in years,' she said breathlessly. She felt exhilerated, freed from all the tensions of the last few weeks. . .years, even.

'You should do it more often. It's brought a sparkle to your eyes.' He studied her, his glance flickering over the delicate flush of her cheeks and the pink, full curve of her mouth. A couple of pins had escaped from the neat twist of her hair, and a few errant blonde tendrils fell in loose spirals around her face. 'A long-overdue sparkle, I'd say. You looked so serious when I first saw you, and now——'

'I think,' Martyn said, butting in, 'that you've kept Sarah to yourself for long enough.' His eyes were dark and purposeful, fixed on Sarah as he told Mike, 'Besides, Jenny has decidedly itchy feet. I've been dancing with her for a while, and maybe it's time you should give her a whirl.'

Mike looked round, catching Jenny's expectant glance as she sipped at a cool drink, and said in a low tone to Sarah, 'I see I mustn't keep you to myself the entire night. I have to leave soon, to travel down to London before morning, but I'll look forward to seeing you again.'

'Me too,' she said.

Reluctantly, he relinquished her hand to Martyn,

who gave him a dark penetrating stare before turning his attention back to her. The music started up once more, a slow and sensual refrain this time, and Martyn drew her into his arms, leading her into the midst of the dancers.

'My turn,' he muttered, his mouth making a firm and uncompromising line. She swayed, caution telling her to keep her distance, while instinct and the pressure of his hand on her back broke down her defences and pulled her towards him. His body was hard, and tautly male, the strong muscles controlled as he moulded her against his rugged frame.

'You're annoyed with me,' she said, feeling his tension in the way he moved. 'Why?'

His jaw clenched. 'When I said I wanted you to relax and have fun, to let your hair down, I hardly expected you to throw yourself whole-heartedly into the thing with the first man that came along.'

She blinked up at him, her green eyes startled. 'I'm sorry if my behaviour disturbed you. I hadn't realised it might look in any way outrageous.' She looked at him warily. 'I *was* enjoying myself. I thought you were too. Has your friend gone?'

'Friend?'

'Perhaps that was the wrong word. Ex-fiancée? Louise? Sharon mentioned that you two had been engaged.'

He shrugged. 'Louise only dropped by for a couple of hours. She and her sister were going on somewhere for a birthday dinner. A family celebration.'

'Oh, I see.' She went on cautiously, 'You obviously get on very well together. Does that mean there were no hard feelings after you split up, or——?'

'We get on fine.' He shifted restlessly, his hand flattening firmly on her spine. 'Are you going to talk all night, or do you think you might loosen up a little and simply enjoy the music?'

She must have touched on a sore point. But if he wanted to push his ex-fiancée to the back of his mind, she was willing enough to go along with that. She had no wish at all to let her thoughts dwell on that long-legged, beautiful woman, who had no trouble at all in keeping his mind focused on herself while she was close at hand.

It wasn't quite so easy, though, to loosen up as he suggested, not when his arms were warmly circling her and she was vibrantly conscious of the slightest move he made, and all the time the steady thud of his heartbeat was vying with the erratic, pounding rhythm of her own.

The music *would* have to be dreamy and romantic, wouldn't it, just when he had chosen to claim her for a dance? It was a coincidence, of course. He wouldn't have arranged it that way, would he? That was just pure fanciful thinking on her part.

No. He was at a loose end now that Louise had gone, and that thought disturbed her far more than she cared to admit.

She twisted uneasily in his arms. 'It's getting late,' she said after a while. 'I think I should check up on

Daniel. Sharon and James will be wanting to go soon.'

'I'll come with you.'

'There's no need, really.'

'I want to.'

They approached the stairs together, leaving behind them the sounds of the party, the chatter, the clink of glasses, the bursts of laughter from people who were enjoying themselves.

Looking out through the small, diamond-paned hall window, she could see that the first flakes of snow were falling, drifting against the dark blanket of the night sky. The bleakness of the scene made a stark contrast to the feel of the house inside. Martyn's home was warm and comfortable, the carpet underfoot thick and luxurious, the wooden balusters and stair-rail ornately carved and lovingly polished. There were pictures on the walls, landscapes glowing with autumnal colours of red and yellow and gold, and there were traditional corn dollies too, in fan shapes and horseshoes and intricately worked lanterns, that drew her attention.

'My mother made them,' he said when she asked. 'It's a hobby of hers. She likes to keep her fingers busy.'

'She's very talented.'

Daniel was deeply asleep in the room he shared with Alex and Christopher, his little body curled up into the duvet, one arm flung about his teddy bear. Sarah gazed down at him with love and tenderness, and planted a soft kiss on his cheek.

Martyn said quietly, 'It seems a shame to disturb him when he looks so peaceful. You could always stay the night, you know. You don't have to be at work in the morning, and neither of us is on call, so there's no particular need to rush off home, is there?'

Filled with uncertainty about that offer, Sarah swallowed hard, lifting her gaze to his face. His expression was shuttered, his features in shadow. Slowly, she turned away from the bed and walked to the door, out into the corridor where their voices would not disturb the sleeping children. 'I'm not sure that would be a good idea,' she said huskily.

'Why?' he asked. 'Because you think there's more to my invitation than the suggestion of a simple stop-over?' His mouth indented briefly as he watched the sudden tide of colour wash along her cheekbones. 'It was a genuine offer. I hadn't meant it the way you must have interpreted it, though the idea does have a certain appeal.'

She was suddenly hot and embarrassed, and her fingers clenched convulsively, tangling with the soft folds of her dress. 'To you, perhaps, but not to me.'

'I don't believe you really mean that. You're as aware of me as I am of you, Sarah. You're kidding yourself if you think otherwise.'

'No! It isn't true.' She turned away, as though that would underline her denial, but he reached for her, his hands gripping her shoulders, tugging her back towards him.

'You can't deny it—I won't let you go on pretend-lng, avoiding the issue, avoiding me,' he muttered harshly. 'You don't really think you can disguise your reactions, do you? I know what you feel, Sarah. Whenever you're in my arms I feel what it does to you, the way you tremble, the way your heart begins to pound.'

'That's. . .that's because I don't want you to touch me. Because I want you to leave me alone.'

'Do you? I think you're lying, Sarah. Not just to me, but to yourself.'

His hands gentled on her, stroking along her arms, shifting to glide down the sensitive curve of her spine and smooth over the rounded swell of her hips. She ought to have moved away, but his fingers began to trace slow circles over the thin fabric of her dress and she felt the heat of his touch run like flame through her bloodstream. Her treacherous body arched towards him, drawn into the warmth of his fire, a sigh trembling on her soft, parted lips.

His mouth captured hers and he swallowed the sigh with his kiss, teasing her lips into quivering response with the slow, sensuous glide of his tongue.

Her mumbled protest was absorbed and lazily dissolved by the persuasive brushing of his mouth on hers and the feather-like sweep of his palms over her soft curves. His hand lifted to cup the tender fullness of her breast and she moaned softly, her senses drugged, her body coaxed into mindless abandon.

'I want you,' he said thickly. 'And you want me.'

'This isn't fair,' she whispered. 'I can't think straight; you're confusing me.'

'Why do you need to think?' He murmured. 'Just let yourself go. . .feel. . .'

'No——' Her fingers pushed at the fine material of his shirt, feeling the power-packed muscle beneath. She wanted his support, she craved his fierce, male strength as a bulwark against life itself, but she was afraid. . .afraid to give. . .to love. . .

Love. The realisation shocked her, creeping up on her out of the blue. Was this really love? Was that what she truly felt for Martyn? She shook her head a little wildly, pushing at his solid chest. She had thought herself in love once before, and that had been disastrous. She would never love again. It was too painful, too draining an emotion, and she wouldn't allow herself ever to go through that again.

It couldn't be love. He had crept in on her when she was vulnerable, that was all, made her aware of sensations and emotions that she had never before experienced, not even with Colin.

'What are you afraid of?' Martyn's breath was warm against the softness of her cheek.

'Nothing. . . I must go. . .it's getting late. . .'

'Did you love your husband so much that you can't put him out of your mind? Is that going to colour the rest of your life?'

'You don't understand—please let me go. I must wake Daniel—I must get him ready——'

'Then tell me. Explain to me.' He held her firmly, locked into his arms, cradled against the hardness of his body. 'I want to know.'

She tried to pull away from him, but his arms

merely tightened on her. He was determined not to let her go until he had some answers. She recognised that and knew that her resistance would be futile, and the fight drained slowly out of her. She bent her head and rested her forehead on his chest, feeling the dampness of tears against her cheek.

'We met at the hospital when I was training,' she said, her words muffled by the cotton of his shirt. 'He was a pharmacist, and from the moment he saw me he came after me. I resisted at first. I thought he was a little too confident, too sure of himself, that he was too used to getting what he wanted. And he wanted me. There was no doubt about that. The more I resisted, the more he pursued me, and I was intrigued by him, fascinated, and I——'

She broke off, then said hoarsely, 'We fell in love and we married as soon as I qualified. I thought it was going to be a marriage made in heaven and, to begin with, everything was sheer bliss. I thought nothing could possibly go wrong, because we were in love and we could conquer anything together.'

She gave a choked little laugh and rubbed the dampness from her eyes with the backs of her fingers, moving fretfully, trying to break away.

Martyn held her fast. 'Go on,' he said.

She swallowed against the lump in her throat. 'It went wrong almost straight away. I had to work long hours as a junior doctor, and I sensed that Colin was getting restless. I thought when Daniel came along that things would get better. He'd said he wanted a child, and so did I, but for him the novelty soon wore off. There were too many sleepless nights. Babies need constant attention—how can you ignore a baby that cries, or needs feeding? There were too many demands on my time, he said. I felt so guilty. I could never be everything that he wanted. He started going to parties when I was out on call. I'd return home to find Daniel with a baby-sitter. It was all perfectly innocent, Colin said. He just wanted to get out and enjoy life while he was still young. . . There was no reason at all for me to get agitated. But he started coming in later and later, and then one night he didn't come home at all.'

Salt tears trickled slowly down her cheeks, and this time she didn't even bother to wipe them away. Her voice breaking with strain, she said, 'There had been a fire at a hotel earlier that evening. It was on all the news bulletins, and I listened, because it was local, and I wondered if anyone had been hurt. I never imagined for one minute. . .'

She drew in a shaky breath. 'The police came later that night and asked me to identify Colin. He was only twenty-nine years old, and it was too young to die. It was such a terrible shock, I couldn't take it in. He'd inhaled too much smoke and at first I was confused and I thought, What had he been doing on the scene? Had he been passing by and stopped to help? It was only when the police asked me if I knew who his woman companion was that I began to realise what had really happened. Foolish of me, wasn't it?' she said on a choked sob. 'I was so naïve.'

'You trusted him,' Martyn said. 'He was your

husband and you believed that he would keep his marriage vows. You had every right to do that, and you shouldn't blame yourself because things went sour. You did nothing wrong. He knew that you were a doctor when he married you. He should have known what to expect.'

'He knew. But he didn't love me enough. And he didn't love Daniel enough. That's what hurts so much.' She dabbed at her eyes with her fingers, and Martyn produced a handkerchief from his jacket pocket.

'Here, use this.'

She dried her face on the clean white linen and said raggedly, 'I'd better do something about my make-up. I'd hate anyone to see me like this.'

'There's a bathroom just along the corridor.' Gently he turned her in that direction. 'Are you going to be all right?'

'Yes.' Somehow, she couldn't seem to stop shaking. 'I'll be fine now.' She sucked air into her lungs and sniffed quietly. 'I'm sorry I cried all over you,' she said.

'It doesn't matter. Stop wearing a hair shirt.'

She rolled the handkerchief up into a little ball, wrapping it tightly in her fist. 'Do you know,' she said slowly, halting over the words, 'I didn't cry when he died, nor ever since, not until now? I was numb, as though all the hurt was trapped inside me and couldn't get out. It was as though I'd thought by pushing it away it couldn't do me any harm, and all the destructive power would gradually fade into nothing.'

'You were destroying yourself. Putting all your energy into your work and caring for Daniel, so that there was nothing left for you.'

'Yes. . . I can see that now.' At the door of the bathroom she hesitated and looked up at him, her green eyes shimmering like bright jewels. 'I won't stay,' she said huskily, 'but thank you for asking. I need time to myself, time to think things through. Do you understand?'

'Yes, I understand.'

She let out a slow, tremulous breath. 'Will I see you on Monday, at the centre? John said something about a conference.'

He shook his head. 'I'll be away for a few days. A series of practice-management meetings in London.'

She thought about the snow that had been falling steadily over the last few hours and the forecast of more to come, and felt suddenly anxious about his having to drive any distance in those conditions.

'The weather doesn't look good,' she said. 'Will you be taking your car down there, or are you going by train?'

'I'll drive. I promised Louise I'd pick her up. She's in advertising and she has a promotion to put forward there next week, which means she'll be loaded down with portfolios and various bits of paraphernalia.'

'Oh, I see,' she said dully. 'Of course, she'll need help with that. I'll see you when you get back, then.'

She went into the bathroom and shut the door behind her, leaning her head back against the solid wood. She felt overwhelmingly bleak and empty inside, more cold than she'd felt for a long, long time, and somehow she didn't think her state of mind had anything at all to do with memories of Colin.

CHAPTER EIGHT

IN THE week before Christmas, the snow settled on the high ground and lay in pristine drifts along the country roads. As Sarah walked from the car park to the centre it crunched underfoot, crisp in the freezing air.

She thought about Martyn in London. He'd arrived safely, she knew, because he'd phoned through to the centre to query some dates, but it was the receptionist who had spoken to him, and Sarah had had to be content with the relayed information.

She hadn't realised quite how desperately she had wanted to talk to him, just to hear his voice, but when she'd heard that he'd rung in and she hadn't been there she'd felt an intense surge of disappointment. Then common sense had taken over, and she'd thought of him spending some of his days—and nights?—with Louise, and the possibility that their one-time love might have been rekindled made her stomach turn over in a sick lurch.

Better to put her mind to other matters, the preparations for Christmas, her work, than to dwell on things she had no control over.

Surgeries were full in the run-up to the holiday, but it was what she had expected. Everyone wanted to be fit and well for the duration, and even minor complaints were assiduously produced for diagnosis and treatment, so that they couldn't flare up to spoil the coming festivities.

Sarah took it in her stride. Only one patient gave her any real cause for concern this morning, and that was Mr Templeton, the bronchitic, whom she'd not seen for some time. He looked pale and rather anxious, she thought, and was obviously breathless as he told her his symptoms.

'I've been coughing up blood, Doctor. It started yesterday, in the evening. I'd been fine all day, or so I thought. I went out for a walk with the wife and the dog, and when I got home I sat in the chair for a while and I couldn't stop coughing. I thought it was the cold air that had done it, but it went on and on, and I realised something was wrong. I'm still fetching it up this morning.'

'Had you been coughing much at all before that?'

'I always have something of a cough, with having bronchiectasis.' He shrugged. 'I didn't pay it much attention, really. You get used to it after a while. But I've been feeling a bit wheezy, you know.'

Sarah nodded. 'Do you have any pain?'

He rubbed the flat of his hand inside his jacket. 'Just here, on the left. It's a sort of dull ache.'

She picked up her stethoscope. 'I'll listen to your chest, if you'd just remove your jacket and shirt.'

He did as she asked, and after a few minutes Sarah told him, 'There seems to be quite a lot of congestion, and it may be that an infection is at the root of the trouble and that all you need is an antibiotic to clear it up. We'd better get an X-ray done, though, to be sure. Will you be able to go along to the local hospital today, if I can arrange for them to fit you in?'

Mr Templeton nodded. 'Yes, I think I can do that. Just so long as I can get back to work this afternoon. Being self-employed, I can't afford to take time off.'

While he dressed, she made the phone call to the hospital's X-ray department, then reached for a form and began to fill it in.

'If you take this form along with you, they can see you this morning. It should only take a few days for them to notify me, and you can either come into the surgery or give us a ring to find out the result. I expect it *is* just an infection, and that the antibiotic will do the trick, but if you should start bringing up any more blood be sure to visit the surgery again right away. Don't leave it.'

'I'll do that, Doctor.' Almost as an afterthought, he said, 'Do you think my work might have brought this on? I've been chopping out plaster and brick in a bedroom and garage extension. It was a rush job, because the customers wanted it finished quickly, and there was a lot of mess.'

'A lot of dust in the air, you mean? It's possible, given your predisposition to chest ailments,' Sarah said. 'Did you not wear an industrial mask, as I suggested?'

He looked shamefaced, and she knew that he had not.

'I suppose I ought to get a supply of them in,' he said. 'I'll look into it.'

'I think you'd be very wise to do that.' She handed him the form and a prescription for an antibiotic, and as he left the room she wondered whether he would be more sensible in future and pay more attention to his health. 'Be sure to go along and have that X-ray taken,' she murmured as he reached the door.

'I will.'

Sorting her desk after the morning's list was completed, she stretched her tense muscles, then reached for her jacket. A knock at the door drew her attention, and she looked up to see Martyn standing there.

'Busy morning?' he asked.

'You're back!' she said, a swift wave of pleasure hitting her at the sight of him, and then the obviousness of her statement left her feeling foolish. 'Yes, it's been all go for the last few days.'

'An awkward time for me to be away. You seem to have coped.'

'Of course. How did your trip go?'

'Well enough. I managed to pick up a few pointers which might help us to streamline our practices and make us a little more efficient.'

'And Louise? Did her advertising promotion go well?' She managed to keep her voice level as she said this, and congratulated herself for not letting her tension show. 'I expect, being in London together, you managed to see quite a bit of each other.'

'From what she told me, it went better than she could have hoped. But then, she's very good at her job, and, if there ever were any slight flaws that might have been picked up on most men—and they are usually men—appear to be quite willing to smooth over them.'

'I can imagine.' Her words came out rather more sharply than she had intended, and she cleared her throat and asked in a more even tone, 'So, how did you amuse yourself in your free time? Or shouldn't I ask?'

His mouth moved in a half-smile. 'We took in a couple of shows. I was lucky to get tickets, but I had to pay through the nose for them. At any rate, they were well worth seeing. We had a great time.'

'I'm glad to hear it.' She tried to sound as if she meant that, but wasn't sure if she'd succeeded when his blue eyes darkened and fixed on her searchingly. She looked away quickly. Shrugging into her jacket, she reached for her bag and briefcase.

'What will you be doing over the Christmas break?' he asked. 'Are you going to your parents'?'

'Yes, we're staying over for a couple of days. After that I'm back here, on duty. What about you?'

'Same here. I'll pick up my grandmother, then we'll shoot off to the coast to visit a while.'

'Have a good time,' she said.

'You too.'

She didn't see much of him after that. When she was at the health centre he was either out on call or taking his clinics at the hospital, and before she knew it it was the day before Christmas.

He set off at lunchtime to make his journey, and she missed him again, because she'd been called to a threatening appendicitis and didn't get back until mid-afternoon. She felt cheated, somehow, empty and a little lost.

He'd left a present for her, though, wrapped in bright Christmas foil, and tied with gold ribbon, and she picked it up and fingered it as though her touching it might bring him closer. She thought of the record album she'd bought for him, the classic that he'd once mentioned he'd always loved, and tried to imagine him opening it on Christmas Day.

Her parents' home was bright with decorations, and there was a huge tree in the corner of the lounge. Her father always took pride in arranging the tree with baubles and coloured lights, and this year Daniel helped add the finishing touches, draping tinsel on the branches, laughing gleefully when the pine needles fell to the floor.

Breakfast on Christmas Day was hot bacon sandwiches, mouthfuls snatched in between watching an excited Daniel open his presents. Sarah joined in the fun, then took a quiet moment to open her own. Martyn's gift was a bottle of her favourite perfume, and, nestling in a bed of soft black velvet, a pair of emerald droplets for her ears. She put them on and

wished that she could have put her arms around him
and thanked him properly.

'They're exquisite,' Martha said, fingering them
lightly so that they sparkled in the light from the
lamp. 'Can I have a dab of that perfume?'

Richard took Daniel on his lap and read to him
from his new Thomas the Tank Engine Book. His
sight seemed fully restored, and there was a quiet
contentment about him that made Sarah warm
inside.

He looked up, catching her glance. 'I feel as
though I've had a new lease of life,' he said. 'This is
the best Christmas I've ever had.'

It seemed like no time at all before she was back
at work. In fact, she slipped into the usual routine
so easily that she might never have been away.

Mr Templeton's X-ray results had come through
just before the break, and she filed them away now,
thankful that there had been no sign of a tumour.
There was only a nasty infection, which should clear
up soon enough with the prescription she had given
him.

Mandy Simpson was the last of her afternoon
appointments, and Sarah could see, from the way
she walked carefully into the room and winced as
she sat down, that her joints were causing her a
considerable amount of pain.

'You've been to the hospital to see the consultant?' Sarah murmured, glancing at the notes on her
screen. 'And you've had some tests done?'

'That's right,' Mandy answered. 'Dr Carter said it

would take a few weeks for the results to come through, but he thought I had rheumatoid arthritis and that he would probably start me on a course of tablets. . .it sounded like penicillin, but that can't be right, can it?'

'I haven't received a letter from the hospital yet,' Sarah said. 'It takes a while for these things to feed through the various departments, and the holiday has probably put everything out. I expect he means to try you on penicillamine.'

'That sounds more like it. He said that while we were waiting I should come back here for more of the tablets I had before.'

'Yes, of course. Are you getting much pain?'

'Quite a bit. I hurt all over. He's given me some splints to support my wrists, and they're a great help. I've a collar as well, for my neck. I wish there were something that would help with everywhere else.'

'Are you stiff at all?'

Mandy nodded. 'My hands are the worst,' she said, grimacing. 'Especially first thing in the morning. And my knees are giving me trouble as well.'

'I can give you some suppositories to use at night; that will help relieve the symptoms that you're getting in the mornings,' Sarah told her. 'And I'll prescribe some Indomethacin modified-release capsules, which should make you feel a lot easier through the day. The tablets that Dr Carter mentioned are ones that will help knock the disease on its head and dampen it down. We get some very good results from them, but of course the treatment has to be monitored carefully, with blood tests and urine tests at frequent intervals. They take a few months to work through your system, but you should eventually find that you begin to feel much more like your old self.'

'I hope so,' Mandy said. 'You see so many people who can hardly get about because of arthritis.'

Sarah gave her what she hoped was a reassuring smile. 'I'm sure you will start to feel better. We've managed to catch this disease at a relatively early stage, and there's no reason for you to fear the future. In fact there are new treatments being developed right now that look extremely promising.'

Mandy went slowly out, and Sarah, glad that her appointments were finished for the day, walked through to the reception office and poured herself some coffee.

'You're looking very serious.' Martyn came into the room and reached for a cup. 'I hope that doesn't mean the holiday went badly for you?'

'You startled me!' Sarah dropped the spoon she'd been holding, and it fell to the table with a clatter. 'I wasn't expecting to see you in here today.'

'I came in to pick up some notes. *Did* you have a good holiday?'

'It was lovely. Short, but very relaxing.' She gave him a warm smile. 'Thank you for my Christmas present. The earrings are beautiful, and you picked my favourite perfume.' She wondered how he would react if she flung her arms around him, but she thought better of it, her in-built reserve winning the day.

'I'm glad you liked it. I played my record most of Christmas morning. Drove everyone mad.'

She laughed, and he said, 'So why the serious face a few minutes ago?'

'Oh, it's been a long day. First day back, you know.'

He studied her thoughtfully. 'And?'

'Persistent fellow, aren't you?' She sighed. 'I suppose I was feeling just a little depressed. I've just seen my rheumatoid arthritis patient, and I know what you're going to say—it shouldn't affect me— but the truth is it does. I hate to see people in pain. It's something we have to face up to, I realise that, but it never seems to get any easier, does it? For me it doesn't anyway.'

'I doubt if it does for any of us. Some just put on a better face, that's all.'

'I suppose you're right.' She sipped at her coffee, leaning back against the table and absorbing the comfort of his presence. He was tall and broad-shouldered and to her at the moment he seemed like a bulwark against the world. She felt safe when he was around. As though life might eventually get back on to an even keel.

She remembered being in his arms, the way he'd held her tight, and wistfully she wished he would do the same again now. Her wandering thoughts brought heat to her cheeks, and she stirred uneasily, hoping he'd put it down to the coffee she was drinking.

'What treatment is she having?'

'Treatment?' She tried to drag her mind back to what he was saying.

'Your patient.'

'Oh. Dr Carter suggested that he might use penicillamine.'

'My grandmother takes that.' He lifted his cup to his lips and took a long swallow. 'Are you free this Saturday? Perhaps you'd like to come with me and visit her? She lives close by Rosenby Pool, and we could stop off and take a look, if you like. I heard it was frozen over.'

Her heart gave a little, unaccustomed jerk. 'I think I'd enjoy that. I hope you're including Daniel in that invitation?'

'Of course. I'll pick you up. About twelve? We could get some lunch on the way, if you like. Is Daniel allowed burgers and chips? Maybe we could drop in at a McDonald's. Can't stand the food myself, but everyone else seems to like it, especially the youngsters.'

'Are you trying to make him your friend for life?' she asked, smiling.

Surgeries were busy in the aftermath of Christmas, and the days flew by so that Saturday came quickly enough. Martyn called for them on the stroke of twelve.

True to his word, he took them to McDonald's, where they scoffed chips and burgers and ice-cream milk shakes, which at any other time would have had Sarah feeling decidedly queasy. Not today, though. She felt ravenously hungry and full of energy, more than she had felt in weeks. Daniel thought it was his birthday.

Martyn was casually dressed in blue denim jeans and a thick sweater beneath a suede jacket, and Sarah was glad that she'd chosen to wear the same. Out by the pool, later that afternoon, it was crisp and cold, but invigorating, and she let Daniel loose to whoop and race in childish excitement across the frozen grass, and through the little copse. The branches of the trees were bare and glittering with frost.

'Don't you go out of my sight,' she warned, and Martyn stood beside her, watching too, a smile curving his mouth.

'Your nose is red,' he said, putting an arm round her shoulders and drawing her to him as protection against the icy wind. 'Are you too cold? Perhaps we should go back to the car?'

'No. I like it out here. Everything's bare and stark, and it ought to seem bleak, but it's beautiful, don't you think so?'

'I do.'

He held her close and she pressed her cheek into his coat and let him shelter her against his hard frame. For the first time in years she felt peaceful inside, and secure, and she wouldn't have minded staying locked in his arms for the whole afternoon.

'I think we should make a move,' he said reluctantly a while later. 'Daniel will be wanting to rush out on to the pool any minute now, and anyway Nan will be expecting us.'

Charlotte Lancaster was just as Martyn had described her. No weight at all, but skin and bone, and lively as a cricket. Her hair was silvered, cut in a short, easy-to-manage style, with a gentle wave that softened the lines of her thin face.

'I've been looking foward to meeting you,' she said as she showed Sarah into the cosy sitting-room of her bungalow. 'You've been at the health centre for some months now, haven't you? Are you settling in all right? I can't think why it's taken Martyn so long to get around to bringing you to see me.' She admonished him with a bright twinkle in her blue eyes, eyes that were just like those of her grandson, and Martyn did his best to look innocent and penitent all at the same time. It didn't work, of course, because Sarah didn't think he'd ever been penitent about anything in his life.

'Yes, I'm getting a feel for the place now,' she said. 'We're usually very busy, and Martyn has his clinics on top of everything else. I expect that's why he hasn't found time to introduce us before this. But he's told me a lot about you. He said you're always on the go, always doing something.'

'You can't keep still in this life, girl. I make a lot of things for charity fairs, you know, just as long as the hands allow me. I love knitting and sewing, and people are always interested in handicrafts. It gets me out and about too, meeting folks. There's too much to be done, and there's no point in looking back and wishing you'd got on with it when life's passing you by. Martyn knows that well enough, or he ought to by now.' Her gaze darted to him. 'Time he settled down with a good woman. High time.'

Sarah wondered whether she knew about Louise being back on the scene. Perhaps, like Sharon, she thought that the two of them had been well-suited, and could see no reason for any delay in tying the knot. The thought left her feeling vaguely depressed, but she did her best to swamp it, helping Charlotte to prepare tea, and sitting down to eat delicious home-made fruit cake, even though she was still full from lunch.

Daniel ate too, greedily at first, then he stopped to pick out all the sultanas and raisins, leaving them in a heap on his plate.

'Don't you like fruit cake, young man?' asked Charlotte.

'Yes. But I'm saving these for Benjy,' he said, beginning to stuff them in the pockets of his dungarees, much to Sarah's chagrin and Martyn's amusement.

'Oh, well, that's all right, then,' said Charlotte. 'I'll cut another slice for you, shall I? And we'll put some in a serviette for Benjy, if you like. Is he your dog?'

'Course not.' Daniel was scornful. 'Dogs don't eat 'tanas, do they?' He turned to Sarah. 'She doesn't know anything, does she, Mummy?'

Martyn laughed out loud at that, then acted as

mediator, explaining the situation to a puzzled Charlotte, and helping Daniel wrap up a second generous wedge of cake.

Watching him, Sarah felt a surge of affection welling up inside her. He was good with Daniel, in a way that Colin had never been. He had time for him, and he cared. It made her throat ache, and brought a strangely hollow feeling to her stomach. Daniel needed a father, a permanent male presence in his life, she could see that. Try as she might, she could never be everything for him, and, even though she might do her best now, there would come a time when he needed more than that.

She was filled with sudden self-doubt. Already in her life she had made one bad mistake, and maybe she could no longer rely on her instincts. Whatever the future held, she had to think carefully about her choices. There was no way she wanted to risk putting Daniel through the trauma of another failed relationship.

Martyn would make a good father, though, and if she allowed her mind to wander just a little she could imagine that he would make a wonderful husband too.

A dreamy smile fleetingly touched her lips, fading as Charlotte noisily replaced the lid on the cake-tin and jerked her attention back to the present. A rush of heat flooded her cheeks, and she turned quickly away, aware of Martyn's curious sidelong glance.

Thinking that way was sheer folly, she silently berated herself. He liked her well enough, and he'd made it quite clear that he wanted more than that, that he would enjoy taking her to his bed, but she ought to know better than to read anything more into it than that, oughtn't she?

After all, he liked Louise too, and he'd enjoyed being with her, hadn't he? He'd said so.

make it a rule that when I've finished a meal, that's it, but it's so hard at times. I feel that my will-power is almost nil. He tempts me all the time, you see, and I'm not necessarily hungry, or ready dropping. Actually, he cares more for his food than I do, and I've always had to cook a three-course meal

CHAPTER NINE

THE new year started peacefully with Martyn taking over the reins of the practice. John Stokes was thrilled with his retirement gift of a new greenhouse, and was only sad that the weather didn't permit him to use it to its fullest extent.

'I'll have to make do with getting my equipment organised and ready,' he said. 'And I'll browse through the gardening catalogues and send off for my seed. You can all place your orders for hanging baskets now, if you like.'

A medical-school acquaintance of James's was taken on to fill the gap that John left, and everything moved on fairly smoothly.

One of Sarah's first patients in the new year was Catherine Markham, whose GTT had seemed relatively normal, but whose urine tests were still showing an excess of sugar.

'I think we need to pay more attention to your diet,' she told the girl. 'Are you sure you're keeping a proper check on everything you're eating?'

Catherine pulled a face. 'It's hard, you know, and I'm so tired these days, I feel I need the extra energy. Since I've been pregnant, I've been thinking about sweets and chocolate all the time. I'm sure it's worse because I know I shouldn't have them. I've been buying diabetic chocolate, though. I thought that would be all right.'

'Not necessarily. It depends which products you buy, because some have a quantity of easily digestible sugars in them. People who are taking insulin can cope with a certain amount, but I think you need to check the labels carefully.'

'Does it really matter that I'm having this extra sugar in my water?'

'Well, it can sometimes mean that you're more liable to have a larger baby than usual. It's best to try to regulate it if we can.'

Catherine put a hand over her abdomen. 'I'd better try a bit harder, then. I feel big enough already.'

'We'll do another GTT in February,' Sarah said, 'just to keep a check on things. I see that you're anaemic as well, so I'll give you a prescription for some iron tablets. That should help to alleviate some of the tiredness.'

'It seems to have been all blood tests just lately,' Catherine remarked ruefully. 'I'm getting quite blasé about them. I had one for something called an AFP test. What was that?'

'It's short for alpha-fetoprotein,' Sarah told her. 'It's a test which helps to show up any risk of Down's syndrome or spina bifida. If we find any abnormality in the results, then we usually do another test, but yours was perfectly normal, and the scan you had a couple of weeks ago showed everything looked fine. The baby appears to be doing very well.'

'He certainly kicks hard enough,' Catherine said with a laugh. 'I'm sure it's a boy and that he's going to be a footballer. He's never still.'

Sarah smiled and watched her leave the room. There were no more appointments scheduled for the morning, and it left her a little time to sort out the arrangements for the HRT meeting next week. The hall had been booked, and when she'd phoned Mike Brandon he'd been satisfied that everything was in order. He wanted to take her out to dinner in a couple of days' time, so that they could talk through the plans for the evening, and so far she was pleased with the way everything was going. She had managed to get a colour-imaging consultant to agree to come along to finish off the evening with a booster talk. She would help to show women how they could make the most of themselves once the menopause was upon them. All Sarah had to do now was to decide on what refreshments might be needed. Something light to nibble on, and perhaps fruit juice and wine would go down well. The whole evening shouldn't be too costly an exercise, and Martyn wasn't likely to complain, since he had told her to go ahead.

She was reaching for her notepad when there was a knock at the door and the receptionist came in. The girl looked worried, and more than a little flustered.

'Is anything wrong?' Sarah asked.

'It's. . . The nursery school rang just a minute

ago. Daniel's had a fall and banged his head. They've taken him to Casualty.'

Her face draining of colour, Sarah was out of her chair and heading for the door before the girl had finished speaking.

'Cancel my appointments for the afternoon, will you? Or see if you can get someone to cover for me. I must go to him.'

'Yes, I will. Are you sure you're all right to drive? Do you want me to get someone to give you a lift— or shall I call a taxi?'

'No. I'd rather get there under my own steam.'

Jenny was on duty in Casualty, and she met Sarah as she hurried in through the swing doors to the waiting area.

'How is he? I want to see him,' Sarah said urgently.

'The doctor's with him now,' Jenny told her in a soothing voice. 'Apparently he fell from a climbing-frame and lost consciousness for a while. He's still drifting in and out a bit. He's been vomiting and his temperature's up a little.'

'I must go to him,' Sarah repeated, and Jenny bit her lip and glanced over at the curtained cubicle.

'He may not recognise you,' the girl warned. 'Some of the things he's been saying don't make a lot of sense.'

'I want to be with him.' She started walking towards the cubicle, and Jenny drew back the curtains to let her through.

Daniel was lying down, a tiny little bundle who

seemed lost on the big bed. Sarah blinked back the tears as she looked at him. He was so small and helpless, and she wanted desperately to do something.

The doctor was standing over him, carefully checking his pupils, and he glanced up as they entered the cubicle, pausing to apply a cold compress to the swelling on Daniel's temple. She recognised him from her time in Casualty, and he said quietly, 'Hello, Sarah. I'm sorry we should meet again like this. We're just checking him over.'

'Is there any fracture?'

'That's what we're trying to establish. I should hear from X-Ray in the next few minutes. Take a seat if you want to. He may not know you're here, but you could try talking to him.'

Jenny and the doctor left the room for a moment and Sarah sat with Daniel, holding his hand in hers. She had never felt so alone in her life before, so desperately helpless.

She wasn't sure how long she sat there, waiting quietly as the staff came and went, having to hold back while they got on with the job they were trained to do. It helped to know how capable they were, these people who had been her colleagues at one time, but nothing could take away the pain of seeing her small son lying there so still and quiet.

A sound behind her broke into her silent misery and she quickly glanced around to see who had come in. It was Martyn.

'I heard what happened. How is he?'

'I don't know,' she said, but she felt a wave of relief wash over her now that Martyn had come to be by her side. The emotion she felt was unexpected and brought with it a glaze of tears to her eyes. For the last few years she had tried hard to manage her problems alone, and she realised now that her independence had been born of necessity.

Colin had never been there when she'd needed him, not through any of the childish ailments or scrapes. He had always been certain that Sarah knew what to do, and that she would cope, and as far as he had been concerned that was all that mattered. He'd left her to it and she *had* coped well enough. It was only now that she felt that a great weight was being lifted from her shoulders just by the assurance of Martyn's calm presence.

'Mummy?' Daniel stirred at last, his eyes unfocused, his voice quivering.

'Yes, darling. I'm here.' Gently she cupped his hand with her own, and he seemed to recognise that she was by his side.

'Wasn't naughty,' he said, struggling to sit up. Sarah put her arms around him and held him close, kissing his cheek. 'Mrs Baker said I could go on the climbing-frame.'

'I know.'

'You won't go 'way, will you?'

'Of course I won't, my sweet. I'll stay with you all the time.'

He drifted off for a moment, and Sarah swallowed

hard, smoothing her hand lightly over his silky fair hair.

'Tracy went,' he mumbled a few minutes later. ''Cos I was bad. And Daddy went as well.'

Sarah sucked in a sharp, agonised breath. She pressed her cheek to Daniel's, and felt Martyn's hand curve firmly around her shoulder.

'It wasn't because of anything you did, Daniel,' she told him quietly. 'Daddy didn't want to go. He loved you. And I will never leave you; I'll always be here for you. I promise.'

He opened his eyes properly for the first time and looked at her. He tried a little smile, then paled, beginning to sway, and said, 'Feel sick.'

Martyn thrust a kidney bowl under his chin, just as the doctor came back into the cubicle.

'There's no fracture,' he told Sarah, who gave a ragged sigh of relief. 'We'll keep him under observation for a while longer, but he'll probably be able to go home later this afternoon if his temperature stabilises.'

'Thanks.'

Martyn drove them back to the cottage a few hours later. He went into the house with her, going through to the small kitchen to make tea while she settled Daniel in the big armchair in the sitting-room.

'He must be nearly back to his old self,' she said, joining Martyn a few minutes later. 'I wanted him to sit there quietly and look at a picture book but he insisted on watching his favourite cartoons.'

Martyn looked at her searchingly. 'Come here,' he said, holding out his arms to her. 'You look as though you've just about had enough.'

'I look that bad?' she murmured, but she went anyway, allowing him to fold her into his arms and soothe away the tensions of the last few hours. He was her refuge, and she felt as though she had truly come home.

She couldn't have said precisely when the comforting turned into something more than that, but his mouth, once pressed in a warm and gentle kiss on her brow, made a delicate foray across the curve of her cheek and found the soft fullness of her lips, pressuring them apart. She kissed him back, her fingers lifting to curl into the silky hair at his nape, her breasts crushed against his chest as he moulded her to him.

'You looked so alone, so vulnerable, sitting there in that hospital,' he muttered roughly against her hair. 'I wanted to take you in my arms and hold you there and then, to take all the hurt away.' He kissed her again, fiercely this time, bruising her lips with passionate intensity.

'I was so glad you came,' she whispered, when she could breathe again. 'I hadn't realised how much I needed to have you with me until you walked into that cubicle. I wasn't expecting you.'

'I'd been out on call, but they told me what had happened as soon as I arrived back at the centre.' His hands moved over her, shaping her slenderness, caressing her warmly. His breath seemed to catch shakily in his throat. 'You can't know what this is doing to me, having you so close. It. . .isn't enough. . . I want more, Sarah. When you're in my arms, I want——'

'What are you doing to my mummy?' the small voice piped up from the doorway and they broke guiltily apart from each other on the instant, turning to see Daniel watching them with avid curiosity.

Martyn gave a short, unsteady laugh. 'Wrong time and place,' he muttered, raking a hand through his dark hair. 'I'd better leave. We won't expect you in surgery tomorrow morning, and I'm out at my clinic in the afternoon. Perhaps I'll drop by here in the evening, to see how things are?'

She shook her head. 'I promised my parents I'd call in on them. They'll want to see Daniel.'

'The evening after that?'

'I can't.' She ran her tongue lightly over her lower lip. 'I'm having dinner with Mike Brandon. He said——'

'That's all right. You don't need to explain.'

'But I——'

'It doesn't matter, Sarah,' he said dismissively. 'It was just a passing thought. I wanted to make sure that you and Daniel were both OK, but I dare say I'll see you at the centre over the next day or so. Anyway, I said I'd call in on Louise this week, and help her move her things out of her flat. She's taking on a new place in London and I told her I'd ferry a few things down there for her.' He glanced swiftly at his watch. 'I'd better go now or I'll be late for evening surgery.'

His face had taken on a shuttered look, and Sarah knew that whatever she said he was no longer in a mood to listen.

Perhaps it was just as well, she thought dismally. As he'd said, it had been just a passing thought, and the kiss had been no more than a comforting gesture that had run rapidly out of control. Maybe Martyn had a strong libido, and if that was the case she'd do better to make sure that she kept out of his way. The last thing she wanted was to be second-best, a momentary whim while he sorted out his feelings for his ex-fiancée.

She took up Martyn's suggestion and kept Daniel at home with her the next day, but after that he was his usual energetic self and he wanted to go back to school to show his bruise to all his friends. Sarah wavered, and decided in the end that it wouldn't do him any harm, just as long as the staff made sure that he kept away from the apparatus for a while.

With his routine back to normal, she went back to work and discovered that things were in a state of chaos, since James had gone off sick with tonsillitis, and some of the office staff were off with flu. John and his wife were away visiting friends for the week, and Martyn was at the hospital for the whole morning, so no one had been in touch with him. On top of that, their usual arrangements with locums had broken down, and Sarah decided that the only thing to be done was to add James's patients to her list over the next few days and take on some of his calls.

If she had thought Martyn might be pleased about her initiative, she couldn't have been more wrong.

'What the devil's going on here?' he demanded tersely, coming in from one of his clinics to find her still working her way through her list of morning appointments. 'Reception told me you've been here till this time every day this week.'

'We've been busy. A lot of coughs, and flu symptoms. And there's a new virus doing the rounds. Some kind of stomach bug.'

'I'm well aware of that. It isn't the point. We have a system that works perfectly well without you needing to be here every minute of the day.' His glance raked her. 'Look at yourself. You're white as a sheet and completely washed out.'

'Thanks a lot,' she returned with dry sarcasm. 'I suppose you think a woman should be told when she's looking less than her best? I was out on call last night, and I've taken a surgery this morning, so it's hardly surprising I should be looking a little pale.'

'I've heard about the hours you've been putting in. You've no business working to that extent. It isn't fair on you, and it certainly isn't fair on the patients.'

She stiffened at that. 'Are you saying that I'm not giving my best? You're wrong, and you've no right to make such accusations.'

'I'll make what the hell accusations I like, if I feel

them to be true,' he shot back through gritted teeth. 'No one can function properly on overwork and lack of sleep, least of all you.'

She bridled instantly. 'And what exactly do you mean by that—least of all me?'

'You're the mother of a small child,' he said coolly. 'You owe it to him to keep yourself fit and healthy and to be operating at full par.'

She glowered at him. 'I am perfectly capable of managing my own son,' she bit out, enunciating each word with sharp precision. 'How I do it isn't any concern of yours.'

'But it is my concern that the smooth running of this place falls apart in a matter of days. You were in charge in my absence, but that doesn't mean the whole burden of surgeries falls on you. Why wasn't a locum brought in?'

'We couldn't get hold of one. There have been so many cases of flu and illness among staff that the service was stretched to the limit.'

'Why wasn't I kept informed?'

'What could you have done?' she queried tightly. 'Besides, I understood that the office staff did keep you in touch with what was going on.'

'I have my own list of contacts, should the system break down. I was told,' he went on harshly, 'that everything was under control. A statement which was blatantly misconceived, and someone is going to find themselves in deep trouble over that.'

'You can hardly blame the office staff for telling

you what they thought to be true. They're under pressure as much as we are.'

'Can't I? We'll see about that.'

He stormed out of the room and headed for Reception. Sarah grimaced. She could well imagine the blast that would follow, and she decided that her only course of action was to ring for the next patient and get on with the job. They must be used to him in Reception by now, and there wasn't much point in worrying.

Things were hardly likely to return to normal until he had conquered the demon that was driving him. She wondered what that might be. Perhaps things had not gone well between him and Louise. After all, their courtship had foundered once before, and maybe it was going through similar upheavals now. She couldn't find it in her to be sorry about that.

Dragging her thoughts back to work, she glanced at her computer screen to familiarise herself with the notes on her next patient. Martyn was wrong about her not giving her best to her patients. She made certain that she paid a lot of attention to their problems, and she was always careful in deciding on the correct treatment.

She only hoped that the HRT meeting would go along without a hitch. She had put a lot into arranging it, and its sucess would most likely pave the way for more.

Mike Brandon was certainly at his most relaxed and confident self on the evening of the talk. If she'd had any doubts about his ability to handle an audience, he soon managed to dispel them. He outlined the facts, and livened up his talk with a video and the use of a slide screen.

The question-and-answer session went on for some time, and afterwards there was a short break for refreshments which had been laid out in the ante-room. There were leaflets for women to browse through there and then, or they could take them home to study later.

'It's going well, isn't it?' Mike said, listening to the bright chatter going on around him, and helping himself to a handful of savoury biscuits. 'I like the idea of providing a simple finger buffet. It makes the whole atmosphere much lighter, less intense.'

'That's what I was aiming for,' Sarah agreed. 'Women need to feel that the subject can be approached without tension; that the menopause isn't an end, but can be thought of as a beginning, a chance to re-evaluate themselves and get more out of life with a new sense of freedom.'

'That's why you've brought in a colour-imaging consultant? To focus on helping women to make the best of themselves at forty-plus?'

Sarah nodded, and laughed softly. 'It isn't a bad idea at any age. I wouldn't object to a make-over myself.'

Mike smiled, sliding a glance over her in a way that was decidedly male. 'I wouldn't have said you needed any help at all.'

She was wearing a dress of soft wool, in a delicate rose colour that added warmth to her pale complexion. Cinched at the waist, it fitted her perfectly. Seeing his expression, and recalling how attentive he'd been when they'd had dinner the other night, she wondered whether she had made a wise choice, and sipped at her wine to hide her confusion.

'You're looking a little flushed,' Martyn said, coming to stand alongside her and subjecting her to a penetrating scrutiny. 'Is that the effect of the wine, or has Mike been flirting with you again?'

Mike laughed. 'Can you blame me? She is beautiful, young and single—or hadn't you noticed? Too busy hankering after Louise?'

'Just remember where you are,' Martyn advised him coolly. 'Too many long and lingering looks and your patients will start to think you're a sex maniac.'

'I dare say it's the wine,' Sarah put in quickly before the conversation had a chance to get out of hand. She could see that Mike wasn't amused by that comment, and from Martyn's tone she wasn't too sure he was joking. 'I didn't have time to grab more than a sandwich for tea, and the alcohol's probably going to my head.'

'You're not driving, I hope?' Martyn said. 'I have my car outside. I'll give you a lift back.'

'That won't be necessary,' Mike intervened. 'I've already cajoled Sarah into spending the rest of the evening with me. I'll make sure she gets home safely.'

Martyn's glance shifted to Sarah. 'Then there's nothing more to be said. I'll see you in the morning.' He turned to go, then stopped and asked, 'Have you thought about getting people's reactions to this evening—whether they think it was a worthwhile exercise, and whether they'd like to see similar events on other topics in future?'

His smooth return to business matters left Sarah feeling prickly and resentful. For a moment or two she'd allowed herself to think that he might be suffering from a jealous reaction, that he actually cared about her being with another man, but she had been kidding herself. Just as she'd been kidding herself all along. There was no future for her with Martyn. They were colleagues, nothing more, nothing less, and it would be a lot less wearing on her nerves if she remembered that.

'I've given out a questionnaire,' she said. 'It'll take me a few days to collate the answers, but I'll see that you get the results as soon as possible.'

He nodded and walked away, going to talk to James and Sharon, who were on the far side of the room. In a moment or two he had joined them in helping himself from the buffet.

Sarah tried hard to squash the despondency that suddenly washed over her. Sometimes she wished she had never met Martyn Lancaster, because then she would never have known these turbulent and unsettling emotions that persisted in churning inside her.

CHAPTER TEN

MARTYN'S mood had not improved by the following day. By all accounts he was more abrasive than ever, and Sarah was almost glad that she'd been tucked away in her room when his temper, according to the girls in the office, had been at its height.

He'd been out on call, then busy with appointments, so it was late afternoon when she saw him, pausing by his door to see that he was clearing his desk and pushing papers into his briefcase. He was grimly preoccupied and scarcely glanced up as she spoke to him.

'It looks as though you're in something of a hurry,' she commented. 'Have you made plans for the weekend?'

She was glad it was Saturday tomorrow, and that she wasn't on duty. She might even, Daniel allowing, have a bit of a lie-in tomorrow morning. It had been a long week, one way and another.

'I am. I have,' he answered shortly, and she thought she might have done better to walk straight by his room.

'Are you going anywhere nice?' she asked, wondering why she had to be afflicted by the masochistic urge to question him this way.

'I'm going to London. What will you be doing? Do you have plans to get out and about?'

She shook her head, wishing now that she'd never asked. 'I thought I might have a lazy couple of days. I was just contemplating having a few extra hours in bed tomorrow morning, though I don't suppose things will work out that way. Daniel's usually up at the crack of dawn.'

'Had a heavy night out with Mike, did you?' His tone took her aback, being thoroughly dry and edged with sarcasm. 'Burning the midnight oil has a habit of catching up with you in the end.'

'What makes you think I was out late?'

'Weren't you? Then he must have whizzed you back to his place pretty smartish, I guess. Not one to miss an opportunity is our Mike.' He sounded thoroughly cynical and Sarah gave him a puzzled stare.

'I don't think I quite understand what you're saying. Where did you get the idea that I went to Mike's home?'

'Didn't you?' He snapped his briefcase shut. 'You weren't at the cottage when I stopped by this morning, and you weren't out on call.'

'You stopped by? Why would you do that?'

His mouth twisted, but there was no humour in his expression. 'Some questionnaires were handed in to Sharon by mistake. She passed them to me and I said I'd see you got them before you started work on the others.'

'Oh, I see. Do you still have them?'

'I pushed them through the letter-box. Haven't you been home at all since last night?'

'No. I stayed over at my parents' house. Otherwise it would have meant disturbing Daniel when he was asleep, or having to pick him up from there this morning.'

He said nothing, just continued to sift through his papers, and she looked at him curiously, doing her utmost to quell the burgeoning hope that he might have wanted to see her, and that her defection might have been the cause of his ill temper.

'I thought Mike was your friend,' she said. 'You invited him to your home before Christmas, yet now you seem to be annoyed with him for some reason. I think you're being unfair, considering the way he put himself out for us in giving that talk.'

'He didn't put himself out for us. He put himself out for you.' He shrugged. 'Anyway, I'm not annoyed with him. I just had a wasted journey, that's all, and I picked up a flat tyre along the way. I had to stop and change it, and I'd rather hoped I could wash up at your place before I went on to do my calls, but it wasn't to be, so that's that.'

So much for the little spark of hope that had flickered to life in her chest. 'What about the repair?' she asked. 'Will it be ready for your trip to London?'

'It should be. I'm going to pick it up now. With any luck I should miss the rush-hour, and I can still be at Louise's place by nine-thirtyish.'

'You're eager to see her.'

He clipped a pen inside his jacket pocket. 'She

didn't want me to travel down in the morning. There might have been too many delays with the traffic, and I might not get there till lunchtime.'

'Oh, I see. Well, of course you're best going this evening, then,' Sarah said distantly. 'Are you staying the whole weekend?' She cursed herself inwardly for having to ask that.

'Probably. I expect to start back around lunchtime on Sunday. I'm on call on Sunday evening.'

'That sounds nice and leisurely.' She tried to keep the dismay out of her voice. 'I'd better not delay you any longer,' she muttered. 'Have a good weekend.'

'I'm sure I shall. See you on Monday.'

The weekend dragged by for Sarah. Her thoughts were coloured by pictures of Martyn and Louise sharing blissful moments together and, no matter how hard she tried, she couldn't rid her mind of those unhappy images.

She did more chores about the house on Saturday, in an effort to block them out, until Daniel grew restless and started to complain, and then she gave in and took him out to the park.

The grass was damp underfoot from melting snow, but they put on sturdy boots and padded to the swings, breathing in the cool, moist air.

Daniel was well recovered from his tumble, and he seemed to have lost none of his adventurous spirit. She had to watch him every second, as he darted from swings to roundabout, and on to the slide, making sure that he didn't attempt too much.

Sunday was damp and dismal, with a blanket of

fog creeping in over the country. She spent the day at her parents' house, helping with preparations for lunch, and spent the afternoon reading, her legs curled up beneath her on the settee, while her father helped Daniel build a garage from Lego on the rug in front of the fire.

After tea, Martha switched on the television.

'This fog's not lifting any,' she said. 'Did you hear that news bulletin? Chaos on the motorways again. People just won't slow down and take care. They just drive as though conditions were normal and then wonder why disasters happen.'

Sarah glanced up from the book she was reading to Daniel.

'Where's that, Mum?'

'I'm not sure. I missed the first part. Perhaps they'll say again in a minute or two.' She listened, then said, 'Oh, it must be local. About ten miles from here, I should think.'

Sarah felt a shiver pass down her spine. She tried to dismiss the sudden qualm that had rippled through her at the news. Martyn would be home by now, wouldn't he? He'd said he had to get back early because he was on call, and there wasn't the slightest chance that he would be caught up in that motorway madness. Besides, he was a careful driver. She'd been with him in his car when road conditions were bad, and she had every faith in his ability to cope.

She turned over the page of the book and pointed out the pictures to Daniel. Her mind was far away, though. Maybe it would be wise to check up, to find out if Martyn *was* home yet.

'I need to phone,' she said.

Her mother looked at her, her glance all-seeing, perceptive. 'Is that the route Martyn would be taking?'

'Yes. It's probably nothing; I'm probably worrying unnecessarily. All the same. . . .'

She couldn't get rid of the tight feeling in her chest, and when there was no answer to her ringing it became steadily worse.

'Try the folks from the centre,' Martha said. 'Maybe he's with friends.'

'Even so, he always has his phone with him.'

James hadn't heard from Martyn, but he said, 'Unless you ring me to say he's back, I'll stay on call tonight. Tell him he owes me one.'

'Thanks, James.'

She was panicking unnecessarily. She told herself that, but it didn't make her feel any better. Then the phone rang and Richard said, 'It's for you, Sarah. Martyn.'

Relief swamped her, and she hurried to the phone, annoyed with herself now for letting herself get so uptight.

'Martyn,' she said, taking a deep breath. 'I've been trying to reach you. Is everything all right?'

'Not exactly. I've been trying to get hold of you these last few minutes. Then I guessed you'd be at your parents' house.' His voice was deep and gratifyingly strong. 'Look, I'm not going to be able to make it back till late. Can you organise cover for me? There's been a pile-up on the motorway and things are pretty awful here. I have to stay and do what I can.'

'It's all in hand. Don't worry.' She hesitated. 'Is it really bad? How many are injured?'

'Hard to tell at the moment. The emergency services are doing what they can, but some people are trapped and it will take time to cut them free. I must go, Sarah.'

He cut the call and Sarah slowly replaced the receiver. She relayed the news to her parents.

'I think I should go over there,' she said. 'I may be able to help.'

'But you can't drive in this, Sarah,' her mother objected anxiously. 'It's dreadful out there. It isn't safe.'

'I have to do something.'

'Then get a taxi,' Richard said. 'I'll feel happier if you're driven by someone who's used to all kinds of weather, and maybe Martyn will bring you back.'

'Yes. Daniel——'

'Don't worry about Daniel. We'll pop him into bed later on. Just take care.'

'I shall.'

Within half an hour she was at the scene of the accident. Traffic was being diverted, and the emergency services had set up lights and equipment and were doing what they could to sort out the mess. A truck was on fire, and the flames were shooting skyward, while black smoke billowed from a nearby lorry. She could smell it on the air, feel it in her nostrils, clawing at her lungs. It filled her with dread.

'I'm a doctor,' Sarah said, when the police would have turned her back. 'Is there anything I can do?'

They directed her towards the waiting ambulances. 'We can't let you get in any closer. It's too dangerous until the fires are under control.'

'But the people in those cars—we can't just do nothing——'

'We already have one doctor in there alongside the fire services. He was first on the scene, and he seems to be a fairly cool customer. He's with one of the drivers who's trapped in his cab. We can't allow anyone else.'

'A doctor. . .' Panic swept through her, wild and out of control. 'Who—who is it? What's his name?'

'Name? I'm not sure.' The policeman looked to his colleague for help on that.

'Lester? Castor? Lancaster, that was it.' He produced the name in triumph.

'I know him,' Sarah said. 'I must go to him. I can help. Let me through, please.'

The officer shook his head. 'We can't do that. It isn't safe. We're not sure yet what's in the back of that lorry, or how combustible it is. That's without the threat of more petrol tanks going up. No, if you want to help you'll have to do it from back there.' He waved a hand towards the ambulance crew.

'But I must——' She started forward and the man's arm came out to hold her back.

'Good friend of yours, is he? Well, he's certainly

a brave man. . .but we can't let you go to him, love. It's too much of a risk, and I'd get a right carpeting if I let you through.'

Sarah felt sick. Martyn was in danger and they wouldn't let her near him and she felt like clawing her way through the barricade. Her fingers clenched into small fists and she swallowed hard against her frustration. She looked over to the blazing truck and sent up a silent prayer for his safety.

'All right,' she said at last. 'I'll do that. But when you get the chance, will you tell Dr Lancaster that I'm here? Dr Prentiss. Sarah Prentiss.'

'We'll do that for you, Doctor.'

The next hour went by in a blur. She splinted fractures and stemmed bleeding, working quickly, efficiently, and all the while praying that there would be no further outbreaks of fire, that the men had everything under control. If anything was to happen to Martyn, she didn't know what she would do. . .

A man was stretchered over to her. Even in the dim light she could see that his lips and cheeks were a blueish-grey and when she checked his eyes she found that the pupils were enlarged. Her fingers went quickly to his neck.

'There's no pulse here,' she said to the paramedic by her side. 'He's stopped breathing. Will you do mouth-to-mouth? I'll try compression.'

They worked in unison. The paramedic tilted the man's head backwards, lifting his chin then pinching the nose. Breathing into his mouth twice, he waited while Sarah pushed down on the breastbone several times.

'Nothing,' she said. 'Try again.'

Silently they persevered, until at last Sarah found a faint pulse. 'He's back with us,' she said, relieved. 'OK, let's see if we can get some oxygen over here.'

It was some time later, when all the casualties had been ferried off in ambulances, that she was able to stretch her taut muscles. She was still kneeling on the cold ground and she rubbed the back of her neck with the heel of her hand.

'Feeling stiff? Here, let me help you up.'

Martyn held out his hand to her and drew her to her feet. Overwhelmed to see his familiar, wonderful features and to know that he was safe, she went into his arms and clung to him.

When she could speak, she said, 'You risked your life.'

'Did I? The man needed help. Someone had to get to him.'

'Will he be all right?'

'It'll be a long job, but I think he'll make it.' He looked down at her, his expression grim. 'They told me you were here, but you shouldn't have come. You can hardly see a few yards ahead in this fog. You took a risk coming out at all.'

'I had to,' she said hoarsely. 'I thought I could help, and I was worried about you. We saw it on the news and it looked bad, but when I got here it was more horrifying than I'd imagined, and I was so afraid. It was awful seeing the smoke, the flames. I didn't know what to do.' Her fingers moved convulsively on his jacket and she choked back a small sob, remembering.

His hand covered hers, gripping her fingers, his other arm closing around her, supporting her.

'Try not to think about it,' he murmured, 'It's all right now; everything's fine. Let's get out of here.'

They walked to his car, and he said, 'There's a service station about a mile along the road. We'll stop off there.'

'Yes.'

She didn't speak after that, her mind exhausted, shattered by the fear that she might have lost him. Instead she stared at the road ahead, mesmerised by the lights that loomed up eerily out of the fog.

'You'll get over it in time,' Martyn said, glancing obliquely at her pale profile. 'It seems bad now, I know, but it will fade. You've had a shock and it's brought things back, but the grief can't last forever.'

Slowly she turned to him. 'What do you mean?'

'I mean I know what you're going through. The accident was bound to bring the memories flooding back. All that smoke. . .the police. . . I know you loved him, but even if he had lived I doubt your marriage would have survived.'

She brushed back a tangle of hair from her temple. 'It wasn't that,' she said huskily. 'Oh, I thought I loved him, but I know now that it was never the real thing. It was just an illusion.'

'Then——'

'I was afraid for you,' she whispered. She bent her

head. 'I thought—I couldn't bear it if anything happened to you. Just thinking about it was like a physical pain——'

She broke off, biting her lip. She'd said too much, and she was glad that the service station had come into view and Martyn was concentrating on manoeuvring the car into a parking space. He said nothing, and perhaps he hadn't heard.

'I ought to phone Mum and Dad. They'll be worried.'

Martha answered the call, and from the way the receiver was snatched up at the first ring Sarah guessed she had been waiting, wondering.

'It's over, Mum. We're all through here. I'm ringing from a service station.'

'Did you find Martyn? Are you both all right? They've been showing it on all the news programmes.'

'We're fine. I don't know what time we'll be back. The fog's pretty thick, so it'll be slow going.'

'Can't you stay there for the night? Isn't there a hotel or something?'

'I'm not sure. . . Hang on.'

She asked Martyn and he nodded. 'That sounds like a good idea. There's a motel. At any rate we should be able to find somewhere to stay.'

'Did you hear that, Mum?'

'Yes. Don't try to drive back. Wait till it clears in the morning.'

'OK, Mum, we'll do that. Is Daniel——?'

'He's fine,' Martha said. 'He's sleeping the sleep of the innocent. Don't worry about a thing.'

They walked over to the motel and Martyn made the booking. It seemed that the fog had caused a lot of people to have the same idea, but they managed to find a double room with a separate lounge.

'I can bed down on the sofa,' Martyn said, glancing at it without much enthusiasm. 'I'm just glad of the chance to freshen up and have something to eat. Why don't you go and sit by the fire? You look frozen.'

'I am.'

She was dressed in a soft woollen sweater and fine cord skirt, but it had been cold out there, and she was relieved to be somewhere warm and bright at last.

They'd ordered a meal—hot vegetable soup with crusty bread, and lamb cutlets to follow. She was surprised at how hungry she suddenly felt. When they had finished, Martyn produced a small bottle of brandy and added some to her coffee, handing the cup to her as she went to sit on the sofa.

'The colour's coming back into your cheeks already,' he said. 'But this should see you back to normal.'

He sat down beside her and they gazed into the flames of the fire while they sipped their drinks and Sarah felt the weariness seep out of her.

'This is good,' she murmured, putting her cup down on to the low coffee-table next to his.

'Yes.' He laid an arm along the back of the sofa

and looked at her searchingly. 'Did you mean what you said earlier?'

'Earlier?'

'If anything was to happen to me. . .'

'Oh.' Her cheeks warmed, and she hoped he'd put it down to the brandy. 'It must have been the shock, I suppose. I'd never have said it otherwise. I didn't mean to embarrass you.'

'You didn't.'

He continued to look steadily at her and she averted her glance, flustered.

'I can't help the way I feel,' she said. 'I know you care deeply for Louise, but that doesn't stop me from I——' She broke off suddenly.

'From what?' His fingers cupped her chin and drew her back towards him.

'From loving you.' She said it wretchedly and twisted away from him, mortified by what he'd made her admit. 'Look, let's just forget I said anything, shall we? It's been a difficult night; it's no wonder I'm feeling emotional. In the morning we'll look back on this and——'

'You love me,' he said. His arm slid around her. 'I never thought the day would come when I would hear you say that.' He smiled, his eyes brilliant with some emotion she could not name, and his mouth brushed hers gently in a warm and tender caress. 'That's the best, most wonderful thing you've ever said to me.'

'But you—you love Louise. . . I don't understand. . .'

'There's nothing between me and Louise, not any longer,' he said quietly. He tried to hold her close but she flattened her palms on his chest, keeping him away.

'You stayed the weekend with her. What happened?'

'She was married on Saturday morning. We're good friends, Sarah, and she wanted me there on her big day. I was glad to see her so happy. I didn't come back on Saturday because there was drink at the reception, champagne and cocktails, and I could hardly get in my car and drive back.'

'But you—I thought. . .' It was hard for her to take in what he was saying.

'It's been over for a long time between Louise and me. It just didn't work out for us. She wanted to travel, to have a good time, and I don't blame her for that. I want to enjoy life too, but I soon came to realise that I didn't want to do it with Louise. In a way, we were thrown together. Everyone assumed that we were the ideal couple, and her family accepted me as one of them. I was glad when she broke it off because she'd met someone else. It saved my having to hurt her.'

'I thought you were so unhappy that you'd decided to stay clear of commitment, until she came back on the scene.'

His mouth crooked. 'I wasn't sure what I wanted until you came into my life. Then it was like being hit straight between the eyes. You knocked me for six and I've hardly been able to think straight since.'

She stared at him, her eyes wide with wonder at what he was saying. He kissed her then, a long, satisfying kiss that curled her toes and left her breathless, wanting more.

'I've been so jealous of Louise,' she mumbled. 'I didn't know I had it in me to feel like that.'

'It couldn't have been anything to compare with the jealousy I felt seeing you with Mike. He was my friend, a colleague, but whenever I saw him with you I wanted to punch him on the nose.'

Her cheeks dimpled. 'Is that why you were such a grouch?'

Martyn stroked a finger lightly over the softness of her skin, rubbing his thumb gently over her mouth. 'I didn't think I had the right to feel the way I did. You'd been shut in on yourself for so long, and when you finally came out of your shell I'd hoped you might turn to me. Then Mike came along, and I realised I shouldn't try to monopolise you just when you were beginning to find yourself again. You needed freedom to date other men. I knew I had to stand back and let it happen but I hated doing it, and I hated him.'

She kissed him full on the mouth, her lips bruisingly intense. 'There's no need to feel like that,' she murmured against his cheek. 'I don't need freedom, I need you.'

He drew in a deep breath. 'I love you, Sarah. I want you to be my wife. Will you marry me?' He searched her expression intently. 'Am I rushing you? I know this could work for us. I feel as though I've known you for a lifetime, as though you're the part of me that will make me whole, and I've been waiting all this time for you to come to me, to make everything right.'

'Yes. Yes, I'll be your wife.' She kissed him again, feeling a thrill of expectation when his hands reached for her, shaping her to him. 'And yes, you're rushing me.'

'I can't help myself. I'm sorry. . .'

'Don't be.' Her arms crept up around his neck, her fingers threading through his dark hair as she snuggled against him. 'You can rush me all you like. . .'

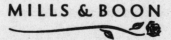

SECRET OF THE STONE
Barbara Delinsky

Paige Mattheson was reputed to be as beautiful as her alabaster sculptures—and just as cold. Her only passion was for her work, until Jesse Dallas came along.

Her fierce desire for Jesse both exhilarated and terrified her. They shared six glorious weeks together at her isolated beachfront home. But Paige knew that Jesse was a loner and a drifter, who could walk out of her life as easily as he'd entered it.

"When you care enough to read the very best, the name of Barbara Delinsky should come immediately to mind..."

Rave Reviews (USA)

MIRA

Temptation

Lost Loves

'Right Man...Wrong time'

All women are haunted by a lost love—a disastrous first romance, a brief affair, a marriage that failed.

A second chance with him...could change everything.

Lost Loves, a powerful, sizzling mini-series from Temptation continues in May 1995 with...

What Might Have Been
by Glenda Sanders

MILLS & BOON

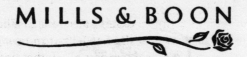

MILLS & BOON

LOVE ON CALL

The books for enjoyment this month are:

PRACTICE MAKES MARRIAGE	Marion Lennox
LOVING REMEDY	Joanna Neil
CRISIS POINT	Grace Read
A SUBTLE MAGIC	Meredith Webber

Treats in store!

Watch next month for the following absorbing stories:

TAKEN FOR GRANTED	Caroline Anderson
HELL ON WHEELS	Josie Metcalfe
LAURA'S NURSE	Elisabeth Scott
VET IN DEMAND	Carol Wood